Praise for *The Su*

"Seb Doubinsky charmingly astounds .... States series and its hallucinogenic Sy .... culture, bends reality. *The Sum of All Things* is a 180-page wonder, bullet style as always in Doubinsky's deadly fashion, a thriller with rotating perspectives. . . . the book is a cross-world odyssey that soars you across anarchist hackers, politicians, kings, princesses and bodyguards with action, action, in a story that moves forwards always forwards. Riveting dialogue and text speckled with moments of genius."
—**Eugen Bacon, *Aurealis Magazine***

"Doubinsky returns with another killer volume in his sprawling City-States Cycle, *The Sum of All Things*. A meticulously sewn riddle that comes together thread by thread, *The Sum of All Things* is a staccato, enigmatic, deceptively philosophical book that will have readers rushing back to the beginning of the City-States experience."
—**Kurt Baumeister, author of *Twilight of the Gods***

"With the swift-moving novella *The Sum of All Things*, Seb Doubinsky mixes textures of political intrigue, drug hallucination, magic and mythical powers with a literary palette knife into a spellbinding narrative reminiscent of the best of Philip K. Dick, John Shirley and William Gibson. Not to be missed."
—**Alex S. Johnson, editor of *Hand of Doom: A Literary Tribute to Black Sabbath***

"Seb Doubinsky returns to his City-State Story Cycle in this thrilling tale of intrigue, aliens, and the politics of historiography. Combining the storytelling prowess and surreal alternative history of Philip K. Dick, the sharp-witted social commentary of Norman Spinrad, and the laconic prose of hard-boiled pulp stories, this novel and the series it's a part of is a must read for fans of New Weird and contemporary Science Fiction."
—**Ben Arzate, author of *The Complete Idiot's Guide of saying Goodbye***

Praise for the City-States Cycle

dystopian politics with moments of frail beauty and the golden hypoc-risy of fame. A wise, witty, disturbing travelogue through a fictitious world that is a mirror-image of our own, *Paperclip* is a triumph."
—Philip Fracassi, author of *Beneath a Pale Sky*

"*The Invisible* is proof positive that often less is more—its chapters neat, sharp tiles in a complex mosaic. It reminded of Simenon and Lem for noir and the politics of a dystopian hierarchy, and reminded of Doubinsky in its brushes with Egyptian mythologies and a weird untethered experience for the reader. Even if this is your first foray into the City-States Cycle, it's as good an entry point as any. Fascinating structure, cool clear prose."
—Jeffrey Ford, author of *Out Of Body*

"In *Missing Signal*, master social commentator Seb Doubinsky pulls us further into his near-future/probably-now European continent carved up not by current borders and bloody treaties, but by the social, political, and racial scalpel cuts of the City States, blending science fiction with current fact in his always intense, sometimes horrifying, and often quite tragic exploration of a doomed race dancing toward midnight, smiles fixed and glasses raised. Dystopia has arrived with a whimper, and no one scheduled the parade. Maybe after the next commercial break."
—T.E. Grau, author of *I Am The River* and
The Nameless Dark

Also by Seb Doubinsky

The City-States Cycle

The Babylonian Trilogy
White City
The Song of Synth
Omega Gray
Absinth
Suan Ming
Missing Signal
The Invisible
Paperclip

Poetry

Mothballs: Quantum Poems
Zen and the Art of Poetry Maintenance
Spontaneous Combustions
Mountains
This Little Poem
Sketches

THE SUM OF ALL THINGS

SEB DOUBINSKY

Meerkat Press

Asheville

ISBN-13 978-1-946154-39-2 (Paperback)
ISBN-13 978-1-946154-40-8 (eBook)

This is a work of fiction. Names, characters, businesses, places, events and incidents are either the products of the author's imagination or used in a fictitious manner. Any resemblance to actual persons, living or dead, or actual events is purely coincidental.

Book cover and interior design by Tricia Reeks

Printed in the United States of America

Published in the United States of America by
Meerkat Press, LLC, Asheville, NC
www.meerkatpress.com

For Christina Kkona, queen of the *Guérillères*.

"Thus they performed the burial of Hector. Then came the Amazon, the daughter of the great souled Ares, the slayer of men."
—*The Æthiopis*

"The sum
Of all things
Is love"
—*Kassandra Alexopoulos*

"Reality is the fiction you can't escape from."
—*Vita*

PEONY

VITA

The sun cut the bed sheets in two halves, one golden, one light blue. Through the open window, Vita could hear the early morning traffic, shouts, a woman's laughter, the sound of a radio, the reassuring litany of daily life. *For how long?* she thought. *For how long before all this is corrupted and gone, a washed-out memory, people will think it's from old films and not from their own lives?* Sitting up in the bed, she combed her short hair with her fingers. She had dyed it a boring brown to remain under the radar. Or the radars, plural. She had changed her looks right before arriving here, three weeks ago—an eternity you could say if you looked at her former life; an instant, a mere second if you looked at the bigger, cosmic picture. Time was the essence of her action—a paradox as she had both plenty of and yet not enough.

The sunrays caressed her naked body, feeling the muscles, appreciating the curves. She shook her head vigorously, chasing away the last inky drops of sleep that marred her consciousness. Her hand felt the empty space beside her, then the warmth of her pillow—her own warmth. How long since she had loved? Longer than she had been loved, in any case. Poor Thomas, Terrence, Paul, Vladimir and Hassan. She had loved Thomas. He had been the only one. She had loved him and they had killed him. The other guys, no, they had all survived—maybe because she hadn't loved them. Love was lethal: it was the essence of death, not of life. The rarest and most dangerous poison. And if, by chance, you survived, you remained crippled forever.

She stood up and got dressed quickly. Jeans, t-shirt, leather jacket. The bare essentials. The hotel room was sparsely furnished, but comfortable—a table, two chairs, a cupboard (painted blue), the bed and nothing else. The smell of beeswax and dust floated around her, prickling her nose. She glanced at the blue sky framed by the window as a painting of impossible beauty and thought about the invisible machine in the sky, the Subliminal Empire's technological eye, watching this planet while it was slowly destroying it.

HOKKI

The plane landed with a screech and a brutal sway, throwing all passengers both forward and sideways. Samarqandi Airlines were famous for their deadly crashes and Hokki muttered a silent prayer to an unknown God, which proved incredibly efficient as they stopped, unharmed, a few seconds later. Nobody clapped though, as they would have in the West. Instead the passengers turned to each other, smiled and shook hands. Hokki did the same with a wrinkled old lady wearing a traditional embroidered blue cotton gown and a flat cloth hat of the same color. She raised her hand above her head, saying something he didn't understand. He then realized she was gesturing that he was very tall, which was true. He was a big man by Western standards, a giant of legends here. He nodded and they laughed together, the tiny woman hiding her mouth with her hand, he making the "ho-ho-hos" of a giant. Grabbing his bag to get off the plane, he told himself the adventure had just begun and that he had almost been killed from the start.

THOMAS

Thomas immediately recognized the short round man who walked into his shop, stumbling over the doormat.

"Commissioner-General Shakr Bassam!" he said from behind his counter, smiling. "Are you coming to my shop to arrest me or to buy a book?"

"Commissioner-General First Class," the policeman corrected him as he made his way between the colorful shelves. "And don't you joke about being arrested. It pains me. Can we go talk in your office?"

"Sure," Thomas said, leading the way between the shelves.

The policeman's somber look was a strange thing to behold with such a usually jovial man.

They both settled in the worn-out red designer leather armchairs decorating his tiny backroom office. He had bought the pair for a few bills at the flea market. The vendor had assured him they came from the Viborg City embassy when it was shut down during the Southeast Chinese world war—the war in which Thomas had directly participated with his hacker group by bringing down a Western Alliance military satellite, forcing him into exile in this city. He was now a political refugee, protected by New Samarqand through his friend Ali, who was the head cop of the city-state and who had helped him buy this bookstore and set up his new identity. Thomas considered the chairs as indirect spoils of war, enjoying their solid comfort with a zest of satisfying revenge.

"So?" Thomas said as Ali made sure he wasn't sitting on the tail of his jacket.

"I have sad and worrying news, my friend. The king is very, very ill," the policeman said, almost whispering.

Thomas nodded, waiting for his friend and protector to continue.

"I am worried about the rumors I am getting. Bad times ahead, I'm afraid." the policeman added gloomily.

Thomas knew that if Ali Shakr Bassam said he was worried about the situation, then things were indeed really bad, as the policeman was prone to understatements. They both stared pensively at the poster of the goddess Nut decorating the opposing wall. She was the symbol of their secret congregation, the Egregorians, keepers and protectors of culture. Founded in 1934, just after the first Nazi public book-burnings, by a group of Jewish and non-Jewish writers, artists, psychoanalysts, politicians and intellectuals, the Egregorian Society was dedicated to fight intolerance in all its cultural forms. An égrégore was the spiritual and carnal manifestation of the common desire of a community, becoming an extremely powerful negative entity. It was, in short, a political monster. For them, Nazism was an égrégore, announced by the cultural wave of antisemitism that had preceded it. The same was true for Stalinism and any totalitarian movement that suddenly seized power through a revolution, be it political or religious. In their eyes, the only way you could efficiently fight and ultimately destroy such monsters was by using the same weapon against them: to build a cultural positively charged invisible "Golem," ultimately stronger than the negatively charged spiritual monster.

The Egregorian Society had moved to New Istanbul in 1936, and after the war had one chapter on every continent and main city-states, each with a secret library, containing manuscripts and publications of authors censored in their own countries.

Commissioner-General First Class Ali Shakr Bassam was the head of the Egregorian Society Section in New Samarqand and Thomas was its librarian and archivist.

"I can make some tea," Thomas offered, but Shakr Bassam placed his hand on the young man's forearm before he could move.

"No time," he said. "I am only here to tell you of the situation and to organize a meeting as soon as possible. I had a quick talk over the phone with our fellow members. They agree that the times are dire. Something bad is going to happen. I know it. We all know it. Who knows what will happen with the twins when the king is dead? What will they do? Is there going to be a civil war when one of them is chosen to be king or queen?"

The twins were the ailing king Ujal's children, Princess Farah and Prince Hamad. If New Samarqand was a relatively functioning democracy, with various parties and a rather precarious freedom of speech, it was also a monarchy.

Allied with the Chinese Confederation, it was considered one of the "evil powers" by the Western Alliance, and had therefore suffered many years from a strict economic blockade. The timid political reforms undertaken by king Ujal in the past three years had gradually thawed the city-state's relations with the Western Alliance, but it was still under hard scrutiny, and the question of who was going to be his successor was considered a crucial test.

"What do you want me to do?" Thomas asked.

"I need you to do some . . . um, research for me. You know, check the usual suspects' emails and such. And some embassies too."

Thomas nodded. He was not only the Egregorians' librarian and archivist, he was also their best hacker.

"Sure," he said.

The policeman got up and turned around before leaving the small room, like a chubby Inspector Columbo.

"One last thing," he said. "Before all the rest, check this person out. It might be important."

He handed Thomas a small piece of paper.

"Hokki Makkonen," the librarian read out loud. "Who's that?"

"Exactly what I want to know," the Commissioner said, before disappearing among the unsorted piles of books.

KASSANDRA

Naila walked into the little study and frowned at the gray cloud of smoke surrounding her companion and official employer, the world-famous poet Kassandra Alexopoulos, who was sitting at her desk, typing on her laptop, smoking her pipe, and dressed in her bathrobe.

"Phew!" Naila said. "You could have at least opened the window, Kassie!"

"I am working," Kassandra quipped.

"You can work, take a pause and smoke in the garden. Here, I brought you a glass of tea. And you should get dressed. We're going to be late."

Kassandra sighed and picked up the hot glass from its saucer, holding it by the rim.

"I don't want to go," she said.

Naila rolled her eyes. "You're like an impossible child sometimes," she scolded her partner. "It's important. People are counting on you."

"It's a just a poetry festival. Nobody cares about poetry anymore."

"*Tsk, tsk, tsk!* Don't be a diva."

"But I *am* a diva," Kassandra smirked.

"So be a diva in front of your audience. It's much more gratifying."

Kassandra put down her glass and stretched her arms with a long sigh.

"Yes, you are right."

She turned off her laptop and got up.

"I will get dressed and sing my poems to the world," she said dramatically, then burst into a laughter, joined by Naila.

"Who said poetry should be a serious thing, anyway?" she asked no one in particular, and disappeared into her bedroom.

VITA

Rule number one:
Never trust anyone.
Rule number two:
There is no rule number two.

HOKKI

"Welcome to New Samarqand, sir!"

A nervous young man in a gray suit too large for his shoulders had just stepped in front of Hokki as he was scanning the airport arrivals hall for his welcome committee.

"May I take your luggage?"

"Er, yes, thank you . . . The museum sent you?"

"The ministry of Culture, yes. Her excellency the minister will meet you after you have settled in your flat."

Hokki followed the man pushing his three heavy suitcases on the trolley. He had brought a lot of stuff as he knew he would never come back to New Helsinki.

"How did you recognize me? You didn't have a sign with my name. Did you have a photo?"

The young man shrugged and laughed. "No, no. They said you would be easy to recognize. A beard. Blond with blue eyes, like Alexander the Great. And very, very tall. Very uncommon here. Not difficult at all to spot you."

They walked to the young man's car in the parking lot, a beat up Japanese model. It was orange. Hokki managed to sit in the front, pulling the seat back all the way. His knees still touched the dashboard.

The young man sat down behind the wheel and extended a hand. "Jalil," he said.

"Hokki," Hokki said, shaking the hand, which was hard and dry.

"I know," Jalil said, and they were off in a screeching of tires.

VITA

Vita kick-started her motorcycle, an old Honda 350 with a tank painted light blue and scarred with rust marks, and began to navigate in the traffic. The streets of Old Samarqand were relatively straight, but crowded with people, animals—mostly stray dogs—street vendors and vehicles of all sizes and colors. She needed to get away for a while from her hotel room, even though she knew it could be dangerous: someone could recognize her and she would have to flee again to another city-state, in Africa, South-America, maybe even Oceania—somewhere she hadn't been before. She had been puzzled when Bruno had ordered her to get to New Samarqand, yet she hadn't questioned it. She was a foot soldier, and others planned the strategy.

New Samarqand was the place the Western Alliance wrongly thought the drug Synth had come from, escaping from a military lab. It was a drug the Western Alliance and other powers feared and passed laws against, but Vita knew it was the key to freedom—not as in a symbolic or recreational freedom, but as a hardcore real thing.

Synth was a DNA-based drug that you could control as you wished. You could turn it on or off as you pleased, behave totally normally, and no test could detect it. Only a very slight dilation of the pupil could sometimes be visible, or a slight variation of your eyes' color. With it, you could live wherever you wished, in a universe that was simultaneous with the reality surrounding you. Of course, it was safer to do it at home, but a lot of the Synth adepts used it basically all the time. Hell, if you could live in a futuristic Tokyo or in ancient Egypt forever, why wouldn't you? For instance, Vita lived most of her time in her spaceship, in which she had escaped from Planet X, bringing the formula of Synth with her, to save the Earth from the domination of the Subliminal Empire.

Synth was not a recreational drug, but the ultimate liberation drug. And her mission was to protect one of the last planets that was still free, although it didn't know it. Like all the others before it, it felt the pull of the Subliminal Empire and couldn't wait to jump in its arms.

But Vita wouldn't let that happen—and that was why she was considered very dangerous, both by the Subliminal Empire and those idiots who ruled the Earth.

NAILA

I watch you every day, Kassandra, and I know everything about you. You hired me as your assistant—sometimes I would say your "secretary" in the old sexist sense of the term: the one who types and gets fucked by the office boss—because I was the best candidate: I knew all your poems by heart, and I could even sing some of them. You thought it was amazing, and you were right: my memory is amazing. I can remember almost every sentence I've heard in my life and give you the place and date. Oh, and what we ate too and what people were wearing. That's how I got the job. The other job. The one I never told you about.

THOMAS

After Commissioner-General Shakr Bassam left, Thomas walked back into his shop to sort out a pile of new books he had just bought from a student who had graduated and probably never wanted to read a book again in his life. The covers were in such a fine condition that Thomas wondered if the boy had ever opened the volumes. All were Western literature classics, considered as the ultimate boredom in these parts. His thoughts quickly drifted to his past life—his computer studies in Viborg City, his political activism, his black hat activities with the Potemkin Crew, the Western Alliance military satellite they had jammed and brought down during the South-East China War, his months in prison, his forced collaboration with the Viborg City Secret Service, his escape and new life here . . . And Synth, that drug he was addicted to . . . That wonderful drug . . .

The irony was that Synth had never really hit Samarqand. It was still too much a conservative society to find much pleasure in living in a fictional world your own mind had created. Too religious too—many considered drugs a blasphemy against the gods and therefore you had to be extra careful if you wanted to get high. Wine and alcohol were OK, though, if "drank in moderation" and in this Thomas found an unsettling familiarity with Viborg City and the Western Alliance city-states. Every civilization had its official maps and blueprints of what it considered its innermost soul and identity, but if you looked closely, you could see how the words were only labels that could be easily scratched to reveal older labels. And when all the labels had been removed, only two words remained: "Power" and "Oppression."

By an incredible twist of fate, Saran, the woman who was his wife now, had been part of a lab researching ways to cure the addiction, and he had been one of their first human guinea pigs. It had worked—for a while. And then, recently, his addiction had come back. He hadn't had the guts to tell her, although she wasn't working in that lab anymore. She was the head of the scientific department at the National Museum. He didn't know exactly what she did, but it was probably something like DNA testing old skeletons and analyzing rusted swords, those sort of things.

Thomas began to write down the prices on the first page of the books with a pencil. It would take him about two hours. The good thing was that Synth could render this chore more exciting. He triggered it in his mind and he was suddenly back in his favorite bookstore, The Forgotten Shelf in Viborg City, which was owned by his good friend, Carlo, a misanthrope with a huge loving heart hidden behind a wall of sarcasm and sad Jewish humor. Carlo himself was there, his feet up on his desk, reading a novel. They waved at each other and Thomas glanced outside the shop's windows. It was raining, as it always did in Viborg City, and this sound and sight lifted up his heart.

HOKKI

"You are a very trustful man," Jalil said as they approached New Samarqand.

The freeway had obviously re-asphalted recently, and Hokki thought, *It even looks better than the ones around New Helsinki.*

"How do you mean?" Hokki said.

"I mean I could be a bad man and kidnap you for a ransom. It happens quite often, but okay, mostly in the mountains. Still, you don't know me. I could not be from the ministry of Culture at all."

Hokki nodded, not knowing what he was supposed to answer. He looked suspiciously at the mountains in the distance and made a mental note: "Don't go there."

"I didn't have your name on a sign, and you followed me. I could have been a dangerous person."

Hokki pensively scratched his sweaty chin under his beard.

"Are you telling me you're going to kidnap me? I am twice your size."

Jalil let out a short but loud burst of laughter. "You have a good sense of humor, I like that! You are very tall, but I have a gun. The gun doesn't care about weight or size. Right?"

Hokki nodded again. The guy had a point. "So, are you kidnapping me?"

Jalil laughed again. "No, of course not. I'm your bodyguard. But you're a very trustful man, I'm telling you."

Hokki looked out of the window. They were driving along the Old City now, which was supposed to be beautiful. But was it dangerous? He scratched his cheek. He couldn't remember if it was dangerous. He would have to ask Jalil.

VITA

Vita parked her bike in front of the bookstore. It was a cute little shop, with a blue facade and orange letters which read *Alexander's Bookshop. Used Books* in English. It was the only secondhand foreign bookstore in all of Samarqand, New and Old included. She had checked. Bruno had told her that it might be an important place for her mission, without any precision. Typical Bruno: secrecy with secrecy on top. She pushed the door and walked in.

The place was half-dark and empty of customers. It wasn't that small, once you walked in, but huge shelves acted like the walls of a labyrinth, squeezing out the space. A man was sitting on the floor, marking the price on volumes he picked up from a pile in front of him. He was a westerner, with blond hair, blue eyes and a stubble that looked like golden baby hair.

"Hi," she said.

"Yes?" he asked in English.

"Do you have anything on UFOs?"

"Sure."

He got up and led her to a shelf in the back of the shop. "It's all there, but it's mixed. Occultism and UFOs. You'll have to look yourself, I'm sorry."

"No problem. Nice shop."

The man smiled. "Thanks. Are you a tourist or an expat, if I may ask?"

Vita shrugged. "I don't know yet. Might stay, might not. I'm an alien, in any case."

They both laughed, but not for the same reason.

"Why?" she asked in turn.

"Why what?"

"Why do you want to know?"

"Oh. Yes, sorry. It was a strange question, I reckon. But if you're an expat, I've got this customer stamp card, which allows you to choose a free book when it's filled up. Ten stamps. One free book."

Vita nodded and smiled, letting her paranoia ease out of her pores like invisible sweat. It sounded legit.

The man went back to his pile of books and Vita scanned the shelves. She suddenly realized that something felt oddly familiar in the shop's atmosphere and she wondered what it was. Some sort of *déjà-vu*, but she had never been in this place before. Her fingers touched the back of a thick volume titled *UFOs: The Secret Truth*. She pulled it out. It sounded entertaining. She found a couple more and walked to the counter where the man was now sitting, pricing more books.

She put her loot on the desk and took out her wallet. He checked the prices and rounded the sum down. As she handed him the cash, she noticed his eyes and suddenly understood the mysterious familiarity she had felt with the place. He was on Synth.

She was smiling as she left the store and got on her bike. There was always order in chaos and she now knew why she had been sent here. Chaos needed chaos before it could stabilize into order. Or even more chaos.

ALI

Commissioner-General First Class Ali Shakr-Bassam closed the door to his office, sat down behind his desk, which was hidden under piles of case files, and lit a cigarette. He took a drag, then killed it immediately in the empty tea glass that served as a substitute ashtray. He was too worried to enjoy a smoke. The king was about to die—or might even be dead already as far as he knew, as Bureau 23, the kingdom's secret service, held all the info. His cousin Sekmet was number two in the service, but Ali would have never thought of calling him: like everybody else in the kingdom, he was scared shitless of the Bureau. It was his good friend Alina Ivanov, the head surgeon of the national hospital and fellow Egregorian, who had told him the alarming news yesterday evening, on a secured line. Ali knew that, because of the ongoing international poetry festival, any information on the king's health would be withheld this week. It was a good thing. Gaining time was crucial. The new national museum was about to open too, the following week. A beautiful building, designed by one of the best architects in the world, Nia Fall. She came from SankaraVille, a tall, severe-looking woman. Ali had the honor of escorting her when she first visited the king, about two years ago. Behind her stern face, she had a great sense of humor and Ali had laughed at her many deadpan remarks.

The projected new wing of the museum had attracted much

worldwide publicity, but it had been difficult to find a head curator. Politics being what they were, candidates had been scarce, fearing being associated with a regime frowned upon by the Western Alliance. Finally, only one candidate remained, a strange bird called Hokki Makkonen. Ali had, of course, checked the man's background: PhD in artistic communication from the university of New Helsinki, various jobs in the field as Public Relations for a wide range of Nordic art galleries and most recently, as curator of the Viborg City Museum of Modern Art. A rather boring and predictable curriculum, all in all. But, even if Bureau 23 had given the guy the green light, there were two small "glitches" that worried the Inspector-General First Class.

First, the guy came from Viborg City, and that's where Thomas, a very important political refugee, excellent bookstore owner and incidentally a good friend and crucial member of the Egregorian Society, came from. It might have been a coincidence, of course, but the Western Alliance was known for its talent in black ops.

The second glitch came from a small article Ali had found on a Viborg City newspaper web page, which he translated through an online program. Apparently, Makkonen had been fired from his job for "mismanagement," whatever that meant. As head of the police department, Ali had to make sure that the city-state hadn't hired an incompetent bastard, or worse, a crook.

He took another cigarette and lit it. Surrounded by an ephemeral gray curtain of smoke, he opened the top drawer of his desk and picked up the Olgeÿ Tazar poetry collection. It was a worn volume because he read bits of it every day. His murder had been the cause of Ali's involvement with the Egregorians. When cultural figures got murdered, or committed suicide out of utter despair, you knew there was something definitely rotten in any country. Ali had come too late to save Olgeÿ, and he never forgave himself. With the Egregorians, he knew he could be a step ahead of the next catastrophe. He sighed and opened the slim volume.

Some people found solace in religion. Ali found his in poetry. No need for spiritual comfort when you had deep, poignant and reassuring warmth. That, and that alone, saved all of humanity.

HOKKI

Hokki was surprised to see Jalil step into the hotel elevator with him. He must have hidden it poorly because the young man shrugged and smiled.

"I have to check your room," Jalil explained. "Minister's orders."

Hokki watched Jalil scan the room with a small handheld device which he guessed was a microphone detector of some kind. Jalil also checked the bathroom and the dresser.

"All clear," he finally said. "If there's any problem, I'm in the room next door."

"You aren't local?" Hokki asked, surprised.

"Oh yes, but I am your bodyguard. Where you go, I go. Where you stay, I stay. Here is your special telephone. It is pink, so you'll have no problem finding it."

Hokki accepted the flat pink horror, not really knowing what to do with it.

"You have to carry it with you all the time. It only has one number. Mine. And if I call you—or rather buzz you, as it is set to silent—you have to answer immediately, or I call in the Special Forces. It has a tracking chip too. It's for your security."

Hokki nodded and put the phone in his pocket.

"Put it under your pillow at night. I can call you if there is an emergency. You must be tired by the trip. The minister will meet you at eight this evening for dinner. You can sleep until then. As I said before, I will be in the next room. You are safe with me."

Jalil smiled and bowed before leaving the room and a much perplexed Hokki.

KASSANDRA

On the way to the poetry festival, Kassandra sighed soundlessly and looked out the window of the car. Naila was driving, cursing the other cars occasionally and laughing at herself afterward.

"I should have been a taxi driver," she would say, and Kassandra would nod.

It was one their numerous routines, the repetition called love, the reassuring territory of shared experiences. The streets of Old Samarqand were crowded, a chaos of architectures, colors, people, things, animals and vehicles. Poetry in the making. Kassandra had moved here after the generals' coup in New Athens eleven years ago. The local writers' association had managed to get her and a few intellectuals a political refugee status while all the other Western Alliance city-states had closed their borders. She'd had problems getting used to her new life, of course. Many of her fellow exiles moved to Western Alliance cities as soon as they could. But she hadn't. She had taken the time to adapt and understand her new surroundings and her poems of exile slowly had become poems of Old and New Samarqand—as the city divided itself. She had even written her last two collections in Samarqandi. One was self-ironically titled *Exiled*, the other *Breathing Through Foreign Lips*. There were things she loved here—the food, the culture, the people's warmth—and things she loved less, of course—the political regime, women's condition in conservative circles, the importance of religion. But all in all, the good overtook the not-so-good and downright bad. Most days, at least.

Kassandra was now the last New Athens personality remaining in Samarqand, but she didn't miss the others, to be honest. All had used their political refugee position to promote their mediocre works, ready to lick powerful cultural hands for a position in some Western Alliance university or newspaper. The irony was the Western Alliance itself had secretly supported the military coup in New Athens. They had "normalized" their diplomatic relationships less than a year afterward, stating that they recognized that the "economical situation had required an undemocratic solution."

She had given a few interviews in which she had denounced this situation, making her the target of Western Alliance media, but gaining her attention and support from other places and communities. Last month, she had been told she had been put on the Clarice Lispector Award shortlist, which was considered the anti-Nobel prize of literature, and actually was much more prestigious.

How ironic that the path of exile had been the path of her fame.

She smiled and shook her head.

"What?" Naila asked, looking at her in the rear mirror.

"Nothing," Kassandra said. "Just enjoying the ride."

ALI

The Commissioner showed his badge to one of the guards standing by the side of the entrance to the National Theater, who immediately saluted him. A huge banner in horrible colors hung above it. It said: Samarqand International Poetry Festival, with a portrait of the late Olgeÿ Tazar as a gray background. Ali was happy to see the writer's face there, but wondered if he would have appreciated the attention. Tazar had been a huge figure in Samarqandi literature, whose horrible murder by religious fanatics a few years back had sent shockwaves through the entire city-state. An exile from Viborg City, he had converted to Mazdeism, the official religion, but had taken its mild and tolerant path. As he had written in one of his last poems: "Flowers can grow on rocks, but rocks can crush flowers/I choose to be a flower and to ignore the rocks." Ironically enough, his murder had resulted in more tolerance and had led the king to pass a series of democratic reforms. Ali remembered his talk with his cousin Sekmet, who had already been a high-ranking officer in Bureau 23. The Bureau had known about the murder plan, but had done nothing to stop it, because they knew it would create political waves and strengthen the king's power, one way or another. Ali had hated them for it—hated his cousin for it—but had to admit that they had been somewhat right. The tragic ironies of history, as they say.

The policeman walked into the building, straightening his

black tie and patting nonexistent dust off the sleeve of his jacket. He was in charge of security for this international event and he would protect poetry with his own life, should it come to it. He wasn't even wearing a bulletproof vest: poetry didn't want symbols, but demanded pure, absolute dedication.

VITA

Vita scanned the street before walking into her hotel. One could never be too careful these days. Accidents happened. She felt the weight of the four books she had bought in her small backpack. Her hyperkinetic gun was in it too, along with the invisibility cape she had stolen from the Viborg City testing center. As her favorite author Jordan Krall had famously written: "Everything is dangerous all the time." She always had hoped she would meet him one day. She was sure they would have a lot of interesting things to discuss.

THOMAS

Thomas knew this was going to be a quiet day. The international poetry festival was opening this afternoon, and it would attract a lot of people and most of his customers. He had actually been surprised to see one this morning, that woman with the short brown hair and the very serious face. Stern face, even. Buying books about UFOs. In his Synth trip, he had dressed her like a French existentialist of the 1950s, with dark pants, a black turtleneck and heavy makeup. He wondered if she would come back. She looked interesting, in a mildly threatening kind of way. She reminded him of his youth in Viborg City and the people who hung out with his hacker group, the Potemkin Crew. Synth suddenly replaced Carlo's bookstore with the Crew's favorite bar, The Zero Degree, but Thomas shifted it back to the previous *décor*. These were times of concentration, not of nostalgia and heartaches.

HOKKI

The meeting and dinner with the culture minister wasn't until eight in the evening, so Hokki took a warm shower and crashed on the bed in his clean underwear. He remembered Jalil's commentary about the pink phone and dutifully put it under his pillow. His tired mind began to mix his own memories with scenes from espionage films. Before sleep pulled the plug on his thoughts, he smiled at the irony of it all: he was both on the run and protected by the police. You couldn't make this shit up. Best title for his autobiography, if he ever wrote it.

SARAN

Saran looked away from the computer screen and rubbed her eyes. She could feel her colleague, Akmet, standing behind her, reading over her shoulder.

"Are these the right samples' analysis?" he asked softly.

Saran nodded and pointed at the top of the screen. "Samples from Tell 2011-03," she read out loud.

"Yes, but we could have made a mistake. It happened before. Not our fault, but some samples were switched and incorrectly labeled, a couple of years back. Before your time, but it happened. Should we check, maybe?"

Saran shrugged. Everything around her felt whiter and brighter than usual.

"The minister will surely ask us to redo an analysis. But it's the right samples. I know, I obtained them myself. And you were there too."

They looked at each other, Saran still seated and Akmet standing next to her.

"You know what this means, right? Or probably means," she said.

Akmet nodded, his crown of white hair shining in the neon light like a fluffy aura.

"Well, the archaeologists will have to confirm it but yes, I see what this means. Or could mean. And it actually explains a lot of things in the tomb. Are we going to tell the rest of the team? I mean before we contact the minister of culture?"

Saran hadn't thought about that. Her team was a mixed bag of people from various origins and beliefs. Some would surely be deeply shocked by the results and its implications. "No. I'll write an email to the ministry. We'll see what they advise."

Akmet nodded, patted her shoulder and walked out. She remained sitting in front of her laptop for a little while, her eyes reading and re-reading the conclusion of the results. Even 2500 years after they had disappeared from the surface of this Earth, the Amazons were still wreaking havoc.

KASSANDRA

When Kassandra walked onto the stage of the National Theater, she was welcomed by a standing ovation, which made her think of the gunfire and explosions she had heard during the military coup in New Athens, way back when. This was one of the PTSD symptoms she still suffered from. That, plus the nightmares. She had to hold her breath for a second, then she waved and smiled. *This is how you recognize the survivors*, she thought. *They always wave and smile.*

The Culture minister stepped forward to welcome her, followed by a woman Kassandra didn't recognize immediately because of her slight nearsightedness. A long dress covered her body from the neck to the feet, made of the finest silk and exquisite motives sewn in gold and silver threads. Her thick black hair flowed freely on her shoulders, like a dark and shiny cascade. The poet almost gasped when she finally realized it was the royal princess Farah, and she hurriedly bowed her head as tradition demanded, simultaneously thinking of one of her most famous verses, "Poetry shall never curtsy to kings". *So much for that one*, she told herself while the princess began her speech after the applause receded.

THOMAS

Thomas decided to shut the store early. He waved goodbye to Carlo, turned off the Synth inside his head and got on his bicycle, a vintage red Gitane racing-cycle he had found lying in the back of a pickup truck on the central marketplace. The price was right and he had bought it, and it was now one of his most prized possessions. He didn't know if it had been stolen, and he didn't care. Morals always stopped where desire began—for the poor, as for the wealthy. But it was always the poor that had to pay the steepest price, and that's where the Devil made its fortune.

HOKKI

There was a quick knock on the door, which opened before Hokki could reach it.

"It wasn't locked?" he asked Jalil, surprised.

"Oh, yes, it was," the young man said. "But I have a special card. It's magic and it opens all the doors in this hotel," he added, waving a blank white plastic rectangle in front of his face. He laughed and Hokki laughed too, to be polite.

"Do you have my phone?" Jalil asked as they were walking out the door.

"*Your* phone?"

"The pink one."

"Ah. Yes. In my pocket."

"Good. Always with you. Always."

Hokki suddenly wondered what would happen if he met a lady. Would Jalil stand next to the bed? His mind shut down at the thought as he pushed the elevator button.

KASSANDRA

"What did you think of the Princess's speech?" Naila asked as Kassandra dropped her heavy handbag on the dinner table.

They were a little drunk, both from the exhilaration of the festival day and the cocktails at the after party.

"I didn't really pay attention, to be honest. I was too focused on my reading. Do we have an opened bottle of wine? I am thirsty."

"White or red?"

"White. I said I was thirsty, not hungry. Look in the fridge. I think I put one in the other day."

Naila disappeared into the kitchen while Kassandra collapsed on the sofa, almost disappearing in a sea of cushions.

"She didn't wear anything on her head," Naila said, coming back with two glasses of white wine.

"No, I saw that," Kassandra said, moving aside to let her companion sit next to her. "The media is going to freak out."

"I think she's a beautiful woman," Naila said.

"I think she's a courageous woman. And a foolish one too. We live in Samarqand, not in New Babylon. Where's my pipe?"

"It's in your bag."

"Is it? I can't find it."

"Let me check."

Naila took the poet's handbag and rummaged until she found

the stinking object. It was one of their routines, domination and submission—although she wasn't sure who was dominating who. What was a master without a slave, after all?

"I am not sure that showing her beautiful hair in public was very smart," Kassandra grumbled, lighting her pipe. "I mean, I support the woman, but these are difficult times. We all know the king is not well, and this is feeding the fire of the conservatives—who are still the majority in this bloody city-state, in case anybody else has forgotten."

Laila fanned the acrid smoke away from her nose and took a sip of her wine. "Still, she is a stunning woman."

"Would you betray me for royalty?" Kassandra asked, raising a mock worried eyebrow.

"Never," Naila answered, bending over to kiss the pouting lips. "You are royalty enough for me."

THOMAS

Thomas heard the key turn in the lock of their apartment and quickly switched off the dark browser he was looking at, gathering the info Ali had asked him to. The screen now displayed a computer game he had recently acquired, a historical non-Western civilization-building game he was quite enjoying. He was playing a Scythian female tribe leader, kicking both Greek and Chinese ass. The door opened and he heard Saran walk in, take her jacket off and step into the kitchen where she filled a glass with tap water. He emerged from his cramped study and met her in front of the sink. They exchanged a quick kiss.

"How was your day at the store?" she asked.

"Short, actually. No customers, or almost, because of the opening of the Poetry Festival. It's the same every year. A great day for poetry, a miserable day for bookstores." He chuckled.

"And your day at the lab?"

Saran sighed and shrugged.

"Not that great. But I can't speak about it."

"How do you mean? What happened?"

"Nobody died, if that's what you're asking about, and I wasn't fired. But I might be. It's a very plausible possibility."

Thomas tried to put his arm around her shoulders, but she shrugged him off.

"Make me dinner. Or even better, invite me out. I need to drink and eat good food."

As Thomas was the house cook, the remark was painful, but he decided not to play the hurt diva this time. He could feel the real distress in his wife's voice.

"Let's go, then," he said. "Good food always saves the world."

Or not, he added to himself. Or *not*.

HOKKI

The food at the restaurant was absolutely marvelous and the minister of culture a truly charming woman. Hokki wondered at some point if she was flirting with him, but he chose to ignore her signals. It might have been the effect of the wine added to the jet lag, and he knew he had to be cautious. He had just arrived in Samarqand, and he had to remember he was there because of another woman who wanted him dead or, at least, in jail for a very long time.

"Looking forward to visiting the new wing of the museum tomorrow," Hokki said with a smile. "Looks splendid from the photos and videos I could find on the internet."

"After the tomb of Alexander the Great, this will place our city among the cultural top ten capitals of the world," the minister answered.

"I want to see that tomb too, your excellency" Hokki said. "I have always looked up to Alexander. What a man, what a destiny!"

"It's a breathtaking sight, let me assure you! All that marble and lapis lazuli! And call me Inassa, please."

"Hokki for you, then," the new museum director said, bowing his head and raising his glass.

He wondered if Jalil was recording all this and declined when the waiter offered to refill his glass.

ALI

Ali finished reading the documents Thomas had sent him through their secret Egregorian network. That Hokki guy was still a mystery, even with the police files from Viborg City Thomas had managed to hack. Of course, Google translate didn't make it any easier or clearer, but what the commissioner-general could read was that they didn't really know themselves who the guy was. There was indeed a complaint lodged against him for embezzlement by the Viborg City minister of culture, a woman named Grete Olsen. Apparently it was still running its course, but no international warrant had been issued. They were probably still looking into it. The guy had indeed worked with two private galleries in New Helsinki, which had both closed down. He was considered an expert on museology, had appeared on TED talks, in television and magazine interviews. Strange—so popular and yet so invisible. Only his public face existed on the web. Nothing in the Viborg City media about the complaint from the minister—just stating that he had been fired from his position. Nothing either about his new job here.

Ali clasped his hands in front of his laptop, frowning. Why did he care? It was a job for his cousin in the Secret Service, not for him. Maybe he was becoming paranoid, obsessed with the political chaos looming ahead. Obsessed with control. His wife called him, dinner was ready. He stood up, shut down the laptop and walked into their small dining room. Faiza was already seated and took his plate to fill it up with a delicious smelling broth. *Such a cliché*, Ali thought, sitting down in his turn, *if people saw them like this*. The truth was that Ali cooked most evenings but had been busy with organizing the security around the poetry festival and the upcoming opening of the new museum.

"You look like you have swallowed a black cloud," Faiza said. "What's wrong?"

He shrugged and tasted the food, chewing on a perfectly spiced piece of tender mutton meat.

"It's delicious," he said.

"I know it's delicious," Faiza answered. "I cooked it. Don't try to change the conversation. What's bothering you?"

Faiza also worked in the police force, in the forensic department. Ali had learned over the years that you couldn't lie to her. She was the Sherlock Holmes of their couple and he, a mere Watson.

"How do you know something is bothering me?" he asked, just for the pleasure of testing her.

"You are still frowning as we speak."

Ali realized that it was true and tried to put on a lighter air.

"Bah," he said. "Yes. Many things are worrying me, to be honest. The new museum director, for one. The king's health, for two. It's like a perfect storm slowly setting up."

"I am worried about the king too," Faiza said. "I think everybody is. I mean, he isn't perfect, far from it, but what will happen when he dies? I hope the idiot has written a will, at least. Otherwise we might end up in a civil war. And I mean that."

Ali nodded. "My thoughts exactly," he said.

"What about the new director of the museum? What's wrong with him? Hasn't your cousin Sekmet checked him out? Nobody can fart in this city without Bureau 23 knowing about it."

Ali shrugged. "It's just a hunch I have. I'm afraid the guy is a con man. Viborg City's police department is currently investigating him about some embezzlement charge. Their minister of culture herself filed a complaint against him, mind you."

"What if he is?"

Ali frowned.

"How do you mean?"

Faiza filled her glass with wine.

"I mean: and what if he *is* a con man? Who cares? Nobody wanted the position, if I remember correctly from that article in the paper. He might do a good job anyway."

"Until he runs away with the money."

"*Then* it becomes your problem. Not before. Eat before it gets cold."

Ali shrugged but obeyed his wife. He was glad he never told her about the Egregorian Society. She would have burst their imaginary balloon mercilessly.

NAILA

You are asleep, snoring lightly. You have brushed your teeth before going to bed, but I can still smell the stink of your pipe on your breath. I get up to write my daily report on you. I go to the bathroom, sit on the toilet, take my phone out and begin typing with my thumbs.

was very moved to see the princess at the opening today. She only had nice things to say. We discussed later on about who should be the next ruler in the city. She said that both Princess Farah or Prince Hamad would have her support.

I send it to the secret number they have given me. I carefully erase the conversation, as I have been instructed to and restart my phone. Every night, I am saving your life and you just snore, smelling slightly of tobacco.

ROSE

HOKKI

"Absolutely stunning!"

The exclamation had escaped Hokki's lips. The central room of the new wing, baptized "The Sisters' Room" was indeed a splendid piece of contemporary architecture. A dome of beige marble and glass, respecting the Samarqandi tradition but stripping it of its legendary efflorescence, turned the blue sky into a magnificent backdrop for the central item—the reconstitution of the famous tomb, a three meters high tumulus or *tell*, as it was called in the region.

He turned to the minister of culture, who nodded and smiled. *Her lips are perfect, oh my God*, Hokki thought. *And that perfume.*

"Yes. Miss Fall, the architect, created a miracle. But it is a miracle for another miracle. Wait and see."

Hokki followed her into the tomb. The aperture was large enough for one person at a time, and the minister went in first, leaving a trail of sublime and head-turning fragrance. *Eros and Thanatos*, he thought. *How perfect.*

"*Et voilà*," the minister said as Hokki emerged in the circular mound, himself followed by Jalil and another bodyguard.

This time Hokki opened his mouth, but no sound came through his lips. It was magnificent, with beautiful frescoes on the walls representing scenes of hunting, battles and leisure centered around two female figures mirroring each other's actions. The blues, the yellows, the reds danced all around, attracting the eyes like artificial butterflies. In the center of the tomb lay two skeletons, covered in a cloth decorated with silver elements that looked like an armor. They were surrounded by a trove of weapons and gold and silver jewelry. They were holding hands.

"The Sisters," the minister said. "Exactly as they were found. Or almost, as the fabric of their clothes had disappeared and we decided to re-create them in this plain fabric, so people could see the restoration."

"Absolutely stunning," Hokki repeated.

"We are having their DNA analyzed too, so we can know more about them."

"Of course," Hokki said. "It will be fascinating to know the results."

The minister nodded.

"Yes, maybe we can trace their genes in the modern population. Imagine, to find descendants of these magnificent women!"

By the way her eyes became dreamy, Hokki could see she vaguely hoped to be related to these skeletons. In one of the battle scenes, they were cutting off the heads of their male enemies. He hoped this wasn't the reason.

NAILA

Naila walked into Kassandra's study with her traditional afternoon tea glass. She found her boss and lover sitting in her armchair, reading a thick and glossy fashion magazine, smoking her pipe.

"I thought you were working on your poem," Naila said, putting down the cup on the desk next to the turned off laptop and waving the toxic tobacco smoke away from her face. "The museum opening is in a week."

"Who are you? My mother?" the poet snapped. "Besides, I'm working on it."

"You are? Reading this magazine?"

Kassandra showed her cover.

"'Today's Amazons,'" Naila read out loud. "OK. You win."

Kassandra shrugged and blew a thick cloud of smoke from the corner of her mouth, mumbling something Naila chose not to try to understand as she quickly exited the tobacco-stinking room.

VITA

Vita bought a sandwich at the corner of her street and checked her bank account on her phone. Her main account, to be precise, as she had a few others, under other names. Everything looked fine. She knew that the Subliminal Empire had the means to trace her, thanks to their international—actually intergalactic—network, but so far, so good. She had discovered through various situations that Synth shielded her permanently from physical detection, even from the Black Shield satellite orbiting above this earth, but the Subliminal Empire had many other means to track her down, as well as the few remaining Planet X agents who had managed, like her, to escape to this planet. She didn't know exactly how many survivors were here, as the less they knew, the safer they all were. Bits of messages here and there, a few quick meetings or phone calls with Bruno—that was it. Loneliness was their best ally, solitude the safest friend.

She took a bite of her sandwich, a sort of caramelized pork kebab in a flat bread with fresh vegetables and a wonderfully spicy sauce, then stopped and looked around before walking into her hotel. She still didn't know what she was doing in this city, and she hoped she would get some info soon. New Samarqand was a lovely place for tourism, with its new and old city both equally interesting, but it was also a semiautocracy or a semidemocracy, depending from which angle you looked at it, with an extremely efficient secret service, which meant she was in potential danger all the time. She took another bite, chewing slowly and repeated the process until the sandwich had filled her stomach.

When she finally stepped into her room, Bruno turned around to welcome her. She was more glad than surprised to see him—he never announced his visits, for obvious security reasons. He was standing by the window, wearing his eternal blue trench coat, creased black pants and polished Weston shoes. His melancholy blue eyes shifted from the windowpane to her face, and he smiled in his familiar Mona Lisa way. In his ears, the customary wireless earphones. At first she had thought it was to keep in touch with the higher ups, but he had told her no, he was listening to music. "All sorts," he had specified—which wasn't much of a specification.

Vita switched Synth to the 1920s, turning the small hotel room into a Chinese-inspired luxury suite. Years of fleeing and hiding had taught the fugitives that a Synth-induced time distortion revealed any Empire agent in the vicinity. Living in a constant present-time, the Subliminal Empire cronies couldn't adapt their appearance to their surroundings and stood out as vulnerable gray shapes among a debauch of colors.

Bruno looked through the window again and nodded.

"Safe," he said, taking one earphone out of his ear.

Bruno was her liaison officer and had become a good friend, a reassuring presence she cherished. He materialized and dematerialized through Synth, having reached one of the highest levels of its mastery. Ubiquitous, untouchable, unpredictable: the three *U*'s that defined him.

"You OK?" he asked, sounding slightly short-breathed because of the crooked beak of a nose adorning his face.

Vita shrugged.

"Yes, but still wondering what I'm doing here."

Bruno nodded.

"It's a protection job. This place has become an important node for the Empire."

"Really? To me it looks more like a nostalgic trip to old school dictatorships. I mean, so much religion, so many portraits of the king . . . Come on!'"

Bruno smiled.

"That's why it's a vital node. Weak structure. Huge underground conflicts. If the Empire wins this one, it will have huge repercussions. You know how they like to play dirty—this would be super, hyper dirty. Like sinking the 8-ball and the white ball at the same time by mistake when there are still balls in play."

Vita frowned. "Not sure I am getting your American pool analogy."

"Well, let's say it's a double whammy of the worst kind. Self-inflicted, on top of everything."

"Whatever. Who am I to protect?"

Bruno handed her a picture.

"OK. No idea who that person is, but you do, obviously."

"She's a famous poet and she is vital for our struggle. If anything happens to her, the Empire wins without lifting a finger."

"How do I get in touch with her?"

"Through the bookstore owner. You already met him, I believe. That's why I gave you the address."

"Is he a permanent Synther? I had a strange feeling when I talked to him. The *vibe*, you know."

"Yes, one of the very early ones. He has a long story behind him. A runaway like us. But from Viborg City, not from another planet. Got hooked on Synth there by our good friend, Dr. Sojo. We have kept tabs on him since. He doesn't know about us and the Subliminal Empire—and how would he? But he could be useful for us. Maybe you could try and recruit him. I will send you his file on your phone."

"What's his link with the lady poet?"

"The store. She comes often to buy books and he organizes

readings for her. They know each other well. Get closer to him, and you'll get closer to her."

"Ok. How close should I be with him?"

Bruno's eyes drifted to the windowpane again.

"He's married. And his wife . . . Well, apparently, she worked on the Synth cure a while back."

"Seriously? The 'music cure'?"

"Yes. They still think it works, here."

"But we know it doesn't . . . Not for the 'forever' Synthers in any case. Does she know he's a 'forever' one?"

Bruno shrugged.

"I have no idea, but you can ask him once you've become good friends."

Vita nodded. "Good friends" had become a very vague notion for her, like an old photo showing you smiling with a couple of people whose names were completely erased from your memory. And you weren't even sure they were worth the effort you put into trying to remember them.

"And why would he be useful for our cause, beyond the lady poet?"

"He belongs to a secret group, the Egregorian Society. We have been tracking them for a while. In the beginning we thought they were one of the many emanations of the Subliminal Empire, but we found out they were quite the opposite. Their goal is to protect and preserve culture from disappearing under any form of tyranny, political, economic, religious or whatever. They apparently appeared at a time of crisis, in the 1930s. And they're still around. Together, we could really harm the Empire."

"OK . . ." Vita said, pursing her lips. "This sounds as crazy as our own story."

"But is as real. I have to move on," Bruno said. "We'll talk again soon."

He faded slowly, his haunting blue-gray eyes being the last feature to disappear. Vita turned off the Synth and opened the window of the familiar hotel room. Below her, the city bustled with life and blissful ignorance, unaware of the cosmic chess-game of which it was now a crucial pawn.

KASSANDRA

Sitting in front of her laptop at the dining table, Kassandra rubbed her eyelids with the fat of her palms. The poem was getting nowhere. She always hated commissioned writing, and the opening of the new wing of the national museum was definitely uninspiring, although the idea of having a special display for the tomb of two "Amazon" women—probably of Scythian origin, in reality—could have triggered something in her. Unfortunately, as the remains were said to be of two sisters, the family picture ruined everything. At least, they seemed to have died in combat together, maybe side by side. That was poetic alright, in the most traditional way. But, her, writing a national familial ode? Seriously? She sighed and Naila raised her head from the book she was reading, reclined in the comfortable sofa.

"What?" Naila asked, always the mother.

"I'm already bored with this poem," Kassandra said.

"Oh. So you have begun writing it, at last?"

"No. It's stuck somewhere, and I can't get to it."

"Amazons, though," Naila said.

"Sisters. Who cares about sisters, except in nationalist poetry?"

"Don't write about them. Write about other Amazons. Nobody will notice."

"My readers thank you," Kassandra said, slightly miffed.

Something, however, had begun to move, like a rusty cog after being oiled. She could feel it.

"What do you mean, write about other Amazons?"

Naila closed her book and sat up.

"There are many Amazon figures in literature and in history too. I checked. Penthesilea, for instance, is believed to have helped Troy and was killed by Achilles. Not to mention all the real ones, like the "Sisters" here, the numerous Scythian warrior women whose tombs are still being found and excavated . . . The Greeks wrote about them and were fascinated by them: they are present in their art, although it was a completely macho society, where women almost had no power at all."

Kassandra frowned. She realized her knowledge was limited, and she didn't like the feeling.

"Hmmm," she said.

Naila shrugged and reopened her book. Kassandra stared at her computer screen. First she would smoke a pipe, then she would Google "Amazons." Maybe inspiration would come from a good old Wikipedia article. Who knew? The Muse did move in mysterious ways.

THOMAS

Thomas was advising a customer when the woman walked in. The young man he was talking to wanted a book on Taoism. His cheeks looked like he had been shot with a pimple shotgun and Thomas thought that his desire to study the Way of the Tao was probably a manifestation of his frustration with his sex life.

"I'm a jazz musician," the kid explained in a heavy accented English, obviously because Thomas looked like a Westerner and was working in an English secondhand bookstore. "My girlfriend told me I could find inspiration in the Tao Te-Ching for my new album."

So much for my stupid theories, Thomas noted. From the corner of his eye, he could see that the woman was now looking at the classics shelf. It was the person who had come in a few days ago and had bought the books about the UFOs.

"So, do you have this edition of the Tao Te-Ching? They don't have it at the library."

Thomas looked at the crumpled piece of paper.

"Oh, that's the Ursula Le Guin version. It's excellent. Your girlfriend knows her stuff. But no, I don't have it in stock at the moment, but I can lend you my personal copy, if you'd like."

"Wow, that would be very nice. I'm not sure I can accept . . ."

"No problem for me. I only reread it from time to time. Just give me your address and phone number, so I can call you if I need it. I'm Thomas, by the way."

The young man smiled. "Amir."

They brought their hands to their hearts and shortly bowed their heads, in the traditional Samarqandi form of greeting.

"Wait here," Thomas said.

He darted into his office at the back of the shop, rummaged through a large bookshelf until he found the volume, and darted back.

"There you go. Sorry for the underlined passages. But at least, you can read it."

The young man thanked Thomas profusely, asked him for his phone number and sent him a message with his name and address. As he walked out, he was already skimming through the thin volume.

"Strange way to do business," the woman said, putting a book back in place.

"It's actually very good for business," Thomas said, walking back to his counter submerged by books he had to price. "I do that often and people come back. New customers. Trust is key."

"Indeed," the woman agreed.

"Are you looking for any books in particular? You know you can exchange those you bought for new ones? I only charge a small fee for the new volumes."

"Smart."

The woman smiled. Thomas couldn't place her age. Late twenties to early forties. Any age, really. With her short brown hair and piercing dark eyes, she definitely reminded him of a 1950s French Nouvelle-Vague heroine. Synth began to rumble and move things around, but he stopped it.

"Oh, you can go ahead, you know," the woman said, with a mysterious Anna Karina smile.

"How do you mean?" Thomas answered, feeling a flash of panic heat up in his chest.

"The Synth. I can feel it from here."

Thomas's brain froze like a computer screen, rendering any calculation impossible.

"I don't know what you're talking about," he said defensively.

The shop suddenly changed into Carlo's bookstore in Viborg City, beautiful and dusty.

"Now you do," the woman said. "My name is Vita. And I'm a runaway, like you."

HOKKI

Sitting behind his huge mahogany and steel desk, Hokki reclined in his super comfortable yellow leather armchair and enjoyed the emptiness and the silence surrounding him. The culture minister had left with her court jesters right after the champagne buffet, and he had remained alone with Jalil and another young man, who presented himself as Hamid, his appointed secretary. Hamid had led Hokki to his office, in the west wing of the building. They had walked through a series of corridors and up a few stairs, and had to open the last door with a special code-card.

"Your security matters," Hamid had said, letting Hokki in.

"Don't lose your card," Jalil added.

Hokki had nodded and gone through the quick tour of his new working grounds.

"Tomorrow you'll meet the rest of the teams—the curators, the security officers and most important, the Public Relations officer, whom you are going to work with closely."

Same as in Viborg City, Hokki had thought. *Good to see some things don't change.*

After setting up Hokki's new professional laptop—a brand he had never heard of, but fortunately used a copy of a well-known Western Alliance interface—Hamid went back to his desk. A buzzer connected the two men, should Hokki need anything. Jalil said he would be hanging around without specifying where, and made a sign symbolizing putting a telephone to one's ear. *You call me*, he mouthed silently, as if it was a big secret. And maybe it was, who knew?

Hokki opened a few of the ten drawers of his shiny desk. Nothing. Just a laptop and empty drawers and shelves. Exactly like his life should be—but wasn't. He grimaced and turned on the laptop, surfing until he found the site of a Viborg City newspaper. There was nothing on him leaving the country. Actually there was nothing about culture. Only business and politics. He switched to a traveler's guide to New Samarqand and checked out the restaurants, bookmarking the ones that seemed interesting as favorites in his browser.

ALI

Ali looked at the body of the woman lying by the side of the road, in the center of the restricted perimeter marked by police lines. She was face-down, her hands tied behind her back, still dressed in the clothes she was wearing when she was abducted: black pants, a black shirt, Doc Martens boots, or some imitation brand. The dust had absorbed the blood around her head. The police photographer finished his series of pictures, and Ali nodded to the forensic officer wrapped in her anticontamination suit. She slowly turned the body around, exposing the gash in the throat.

Ali already knew who she was. He had seen the video of her execution that was sent earlier in the morning by the Mazdeic Watchmen, or whatever they were called. Mariam Sumarova, thirty-eight years old, painter and member of the National Academy. She'd had an exhibit a few weeks ago that had generated some scandal and disproportionate media attention: nude men, painted in a hyperrealist style, front facing. The conservative parties and the religious congregations had gone amok, some calling for her firing from the institution, others for a prison stint for "deliberate obscenity" and a few for her death. Apparently the last ones had been heard.

The Commissioner-General First Class sadly shook his head. When artists, poets and writers were getting murdered, you knew bad things were happening. And as an Egregorian, he knew what that meant: negative energies of the highest kind were gathering in order to launch a devastating attack on this city.

The sound of an approaching car made him turn his head. An unmarked black car was approaching in a small cloud of dust. Bureau 23, no doubt. They would probably want to take over this case. All the better. Ali didn't want to appear on some terrorist organization's death-list. And, as an Egregorian, he had other means to investigate.

VITA

So the young bookseller's name was Thomas, like the only person Vita had ever loved. The strange and meaningless coincidences of life. She enjoyed the panic in his eyes, the lies his lips were forming, the denial shaped with his hands—not that she was cruel, no. Merciless, yes, she could be. And she had to be: the Subliminal Empire had killed too many of her friends and allies. The times were not of compassion.

"Are you working for the Viborg City secret service?" he finally asked.

"I was," Vita admitted. "But not anymore."

Carlo's bookstore flickered and disappeared, and Thomas nodded in silence.

"Maybe we should go into my office and talk," he said.

"I was just about to suggest the same thing," Vita said. "Synchronicity."

SARAN

"So," Akmet said, "here we are."

Saran nodded. They were both standing in front of Saran's desk in her little office, staring at her laptop.

"Yes. Here we are."

The ministry of culture's email was clear: hold back the genetic test results until after the official opening of the new wing of the national museum.

"Makes sense," Akmet approved, caressing his gray stubble. "I would have done the same."

"Yes, I would have too, given the circumstances."

"Politics," Akmet said.

"Politics *and* science," Saran added. "Never a good match, one way or another."

"Should we take a tea break?"

Saran nodded. "Good idea."

The cafeteria was empty, and they sat facing each other at one of the tables.

"We need to forward the message to the team. Let them know they must keep the result under wraps for now," Saran said, softly blowing on the surface of the scorching amber liquid.

"We also have to plan what we're going to say later, when we publish the results."

"Oh my God," she sighed. "Didn't think about that. You're right. I have to call the minister's office about this."

Thoughts whirled in her head, mimicking the tea's vapor.

"Some people are going to be really pissed off. They might even want to shut down that part of the museum," she said.

"I always said that this genetic test was a bad idea," Akmet said. "I warned you against it. Especially sending it to a foreign lab. It's all in our email exchanges. As the head of our section, the whole roof might fall on you. I want no part of it."

Saran felt a knot form in her stomach. Akmet was right. And he was telling her now that he was going to let her sink, without lifting a finger. He had always wanted her position. He resented her being younger and a woman—had said it many times. It was his big chance now.

"I agreed with you, but I had to obey the minister. It's also in the emails. I explained this many times. We are not free to do what we want. It's politics. Only politics."

A small group of colleagues walked into the cafeteria and Saran stood up.

"Work is calling," she excused herself.

"Let me know what the minister says when you've talked to her," Akmet said, with a wink.

It wasn't a friendly wink. It was an ominous one.

Saran hurried back to her office, her blood pulsing violently in her temples, feeling a panic attack building up in her agitated mind.

Sitting behind her desk, she unlocked her bottom drawer and nervously searched for her Mindfulness Helper pills. She took two and washed them down with bottled mineral water. Closing her eyes, she waited for the pills to fulfill their purpose. Soon, peace would come, soon the panic would disappear, soon she would be herself again—a totally focused functioning human being capable of facing one of the biggest shitstorms she would probably ever know.

HOKKI

Hokki was hungry and he buzzed Hamid.

"Sir?"

"I'm hungry. Any good place to eat?"

"Well, there's the cafeteria . . ."

"I said a "good place"."

"Just a minute, sir."

The door opened. Jalil stepped in instead of Hamid. *Of course,* Hokki thought but he managed to smile despite his irritation.

"I know a place," the young man said.

The restaurant was a few streets away from the museum. It was tiny, dark and crowded, but wonderful smells tickled Hokki's nostrils and his stomach growled in contentment.

"I have no idea about the local cuisine," Hokki said once they were seated. "And the menu is in Samarqandi. What do you recommend?"

"A *palov,* definitely. It's our national dish. It's like a pilaf, with mutton and vegetables. Spicy. Excellent."

Excellent indeed, Hokki later thought, scraping the last bits with a delicious chunk of mellow bread.

"So, tell me a little bit more about yourself, Jalil," he said, after ordering a strong Turkish coffee.

"Not much to say. I joined the police because I was poor. I am still poor, but I am in the police."

He smiled and Hokki felt that the conversation was over.

Hokki nodded, paid for the meal and they left.

They walked silently on the way back to the museum, like an old couple that had failed to save their marriage.

KASSANDRA

"Naila, darling, can you lend me the books on the Amazons you said you've read? I can't find them in the shelves! Are they in your room?"

"I didn't read any books," Naila shouted back from the sitting room where she was watching a television program on New Babylon's thriving new restaurant scene. "I looked up Amazons on the Net!"

"Ah . . ."

Kassandra turned on her laptop and Googled the word. 728,000 hits. Grabbing a pen and a paper block, she began to write down some book references. She felt a little bit ashamed of her own ignorance, although she would never have admitted it, even to her own reflection in the mirror. But, of course, one cannot know everything. Not even poets. *Especially not poets*, she mentally rectified.

She checked the national library site to see if they carried any of the titles, but none were registered.

Of course, she thought. *Fucking patriarchal society.*

She sat for a while in front of the screen, mulling over her options. She had to write and publicly read her poem next week for the opening of the new wing of the National Museum where the Amazon sisters' tomb was going to be displayed—which meant exactly ten days from now. It was supposed to be a ten-minute read, around twenty-five pages give or take. And, at this very moment, she had written nothing, zero, zilch.

She glanced at the search results in front of her. There were quite a few articles, but she hated to read on screen.

Then she remembered that the English secondhand bookstore had a whole section on Women's History and she considered Thomas, the owner or manager, as a good friend. She would pay him a visit. Maybe he could save her day.

"I am going out!" she yelled as she put on her coat.

"Where are you going?" Naila yelled back from the kitchen where she was boiling some water for her early afternoon tea.

"To find some Amazons!"

"Good luck! Don't let them shoot arrows in your ass!"

Kassandra had to laugh. Naila's humor was terrible. She loved it.

HOKKI

Looking out of his office window, Hokki admired the view. The Blue Mosque's golden dome shone in the distance, one of the many holy buildings of the city. Before leaving Viborg City, he had read quite a lot about New Samarqand, which had been known for being a cross-cultural center for many centuries. What ancient Rome had been once, Samarqand was still today: clothes, languages, food, music, everything was colorful and varied. But here, as he understood, religions drew invisible borders and territories. The king was the symbolic head of the Revealed Word of Mazdeism, which was the state religion. But, like all beliefs, it seemed that there were many currents, from open-minded to conservative, and more. In the past few years, according to the Wikipedia entry, the city-state had known some terror episodes linked with ultra-Mazdeist groups. The position of the king had been ambivalent on the subject, and had attracted staunch criticism from the Western Alliance countries. The fact that New Samarqand had also been a diplomatic ally of the Chinese Confederation during the latest conflict had, of course, not helped.

And here Hokki was today, running away from his past, ready for the most uncertain future. *A pariah in a pariah land*, he thought. *What's not to like?*

THOMAS

"So . . ." Thomas sighed as he and the woman who had introduced herself as Vita sat down on opposite sides of his desk. "Who are you? How did you find me? What do you want?"

Vita, if that was her real name, shrugged and shook her head.

"Questions, questions, questions. You men are all the same," she said with a smirk.

When she made the face, Thomas suddenly realized how beautiful she was—but of a strange kind of beauty, as if it morphed all the time between plain and stunning.

"Just kidding," she said. "Sorry."

"What happened out there? I mean in the shop? We were together in my vision . . . The Forgotten Shelves in Viborg City . . . How is that possible?"

"Shared Synth vibrations," Vita calmly explained as Thomas felt a wind of panic gallop along his spine. "You didn't even know you could do that, right?

Synth is fueled by memories—all our memories, real or imagined. What we have lived, experienced, read, seen, listened to, enjoyed. Everything. We both know that place. We have both been in the bookstore, talked to Carlo, bought secondhand books, drunk his abominable mint-tea . . ."

Thomas involuntarily smiled at the memory. It was true: that dark mixture Carlo called "mint-tea" could definitely kill the unsuspecting victim.

"And if we have the same memories or imbed references, Synth can put us on the same mind wavelength, so we can share."

Thomas frowned. "You really *are* an agent from Viborg City then?"

"No. I was."

"And you got hooked on Synth there?"

Vita's eyes narrowed and she took a few seconds to answer.

"I brought Synth there. Or rather, a friend of mine did. You knew him: Dr. Sojo."

Thomas felt his panic go up a notch. She did seem to know an awful lot about him. Dr. Sojo was his dealer in Viborg City. And a friend. Sort of. At least someone whose company he had enjoyed in his isolated life back then.

"What else do you know?"

"You were a member of the anarchist hacker group called the Potemkin Crew, and you sabotaged a Western alliance military satellite during the South-East China conflict. You were later arrested and forced to work for the Viborg City intelligence agency as a white hat. Then you fled and came here. And you are still on Viborg City's top ten most-wanted list."

Thomas was speechless.

"I did my research," Vita added, with the proud smile of a top-notch student.

Thomas felt an invisible ceiling of incredible weight fall down on his shoulders. He thought of Saran, of the new life he had managed to build here for himself, with the help of his friend, Ali, and the Egregorian society. He had woken up today feeling glad about his work, loving this city, loving his wife in spite of their problems, and now . . .

"I don't have a gun," he said, lifting his hands up in the air. "I won't resist if you arrest me. Just let me warn my wife. Let me call her."

"Oh, so dramatic!" Vita laughed. "I am *not* here to arrest you. I told you I was a fugitive too. You're not a very good listener, Thomas."

Thoughts exploded in Thomas's brain like two planes crashing into each other on the tarmac.

"I don't understand. What do you want?"

"To make it simple: I want to become your friend."

"You know this sounds very strange and even suspicious, right?"

Vita nodded and Thomas felt a conflicting mix of confidence and distrust churn in his guts. He had been part of an underground movement; he had been betrayed and sent to jail. He had seen how the system could force you to collaborate and use you as it wanted. The system had made it impossible to trust anyone completely—even Saran, even Ali, even the members of the Egregorian Society. He was always waiting for the police to come knocking at his door at three a.m. in the morning.

"Okay, maybe a friend is too much to ask for," Vita resumed as if she had read his mind. "How about an ally then?"

"An ally? To do what?"

"To protect this place."

Thomas scratched his stubble. The rough skin under his fingers was reassuringly real.

"What place? This bookstore? New Samarqand?"

"This place you call Earth, silly. This entire place."

There was a sudden knock on the door, and it opened before Thomas could say anything. A woman's face appeared in the doorway.

"Sorry! I didn't want to interrupt anything!"

Thomas recognized his good friend Kassandra Alexopoulos, the poetess who often came by to buy books and discuss literature and politics. He stood up to greet her, happy for the interruption.

Vita stood up too and made her way around them.

"I'll come back later," she said. "We have a lot of things to talk about."

"Who is she?" Kassandra asked as Vita disappeared between the shelves and walked out to the sound of the door's tiny bell.

Thomas shrugged.

"I don't really know, to be honest. She says she comes from my home city and I think she might be completely crazy."

"Bad crazy or good crazy?"

"I'm not sure. That's the problem. What can I help you with?"

ALI

Commissioner-General Ali Shakr Bassam had just walked into his office when his mobile phone rang. He recognized his cousin Sekmet's private number, if a Bureau 23 high-ranking officer could actually have a "private" number. Knowing that everything they would say would certainly be monitored and processed, he carefully closed his door, sat behind his desk and answered the call.

"Ali?"

"Sekmet?"

"You can talk?"

"Yes. I'm alone in my office."

Ali wondered why Sekmet would ask such a stupid question when he knew perfectly well their conversation was being recorded on some government's server.

"Mariam Sumarova," Sekmet resumed. "I was told you were there."

"Yes."

There was a short silence on the other end of the line. A hesitation, maybe?

"What do you make of it?"

"Well, the Mazdeic Watchmen sent the video of her murder, so I make it they killed her."

"The Guardians of Mazda," Skemet corrected him. "Yes. I

know that. But I want your thoughts on this. You are a clever man. I am going to tell you something that must remain between us."

Silence again. *Between us and twenty Bureau 23 officers*, Ali thought. *Whatever.* The silence lasted.

"Sekmet?"

"The king is dying."

"Oh!"

Ali acted surprised. He had to protect his source at the hospital who had given him the king's status a couple of days ago.

"That is bad news," he added, to sound even more convincing.

"Yes. Very. But it's even worse than you think. The king has been placed in an artificial coma since last night. And he hasn't written his will."

This time it was Ali's turn to become silent. The queen had died a few years ago and with no will, there could be—would be—a dynastic crisis, as no one knew which of the twin heirs would sit on the throne.

"You're sure about the will?" the commissioner finally resumed.

"Yes. We have direct access to that sort of information."

"Hmmm. But couldn't you, I don't know, *produce* a will?"

Sekmet had a short laugh. "We might be rotten, Ali, but we're not *that* rotten. And what's more, who would we choose? And who would decide who we choose? We are as split as all the citizens of this city-state."

Alone in his office, Ali nodded. The choice was tough indeed. It was as if the king's personality had split into two different incarnations: Crown Princess Farah represented the possibility of a political opening with the Western Alliance, but many feared that it would bring foreign corruption and "bad habits" within the kingdom; Crown Prince Hamad, on the contrary, was very pious and conservative, and others saw him as a threat to the normalization of the diplomatic relationships begun by his father and the implementation of more rigorous religious politics. For the first time in his life, Ali almost wished he was a republican, because both doors seemed to lead to a certain political doom for New Samarqand.

"How does this relate to Mariam Sumarova's murder?" he finally asked, trying to get the conversation back on its original track.

"I don't know if it does. That's why I'm asking you. You're one the best cops I know, and I'm not saying that because we are family. I need a fresh look on these terrorists. Someone who can examine things from the outside in, and whose judgment I trust."

"This month is very cultural—there are exhibits, the international poetry festival, the opening of the new wing of the National Museum. Lots of events to irritate the fanatics. Ideal times for political unrest. If the royal kids know their father is dying, they're going to play every dirty trick possible to gain support. We know the Prime Minister is close to Princess Farah—she has always supported his party. The murder puts him in a tough position, with all the international attention we are getting. But would Prince Hamad support a terrorist group? I am not sure. In any case, I would consider the group as a third player in all this. Even if Hamad is behind them, one way or another."

"Yes, I would agree on this," Sekmet said. "I just wanted to hear it from you. I have a suggestion."

That sounds bad, Ali thought.

"Yes?"

"Let's work closely together, until the skies are cleared."

Very bad indeed. But I have no choice.

"Sure."

"Just you and me, nobody else involved."

Except all those listening to us right now.

"We exchange info," Sekmet continued. "All the info we have. Sources too. Everything."

So that's what you wanted from the start, dear cousin. My sources. Clever, clever. The king is definitely dying and Bureau

23 is getting ready to do anything to retain political control over an uncertain future. You get the criminal informants, you get the whole network.

"Sure," Ali said.

"Excellent. You can always reach me at this number."

Sekmet hung up and Ali made an obscene gesture to no one in particular in the emptiness of his office, which made him feel a lot better and even brought a smile to his face.

HOKKI

"Sir!"

"Yes, Jalil?"

"Where are you going?"

"Well, I am officially the director of this museum, but I haven't visited it yet. I mean, the new wing, yes. But not the rest. So I'm going to get cultured."

Hokki was standing in the lobby in front of his office. Jalil put aside the newspaper he was reading and stood up from the designer armchair he was sitting in. The chair was small and didn't look very comfortable. Jalil winced and stretched, as if to confirm Hokki's thoughts.

"You're going to sit here all day?"

Jalil nodded. "Except when I have to go to the bathroom, of course. Or to accompany you wherever you want to go."

Hokki smiled, but Jalil's face remained serious.

"It doesn't look very comfortable."

Jalil shrugged. Hokki decided to try it for himself and got stuck half-way down. His ass couldn't fit in. Jalil helped him back up.

"Not made for a giant," the bodyguard said.

Hamid, the secretary, who had been watching the scene from behind his desk, chuckled discreetly.

"I'll get you another one," Hokki said, slapping the side of his burning thighs. "Hamid, can you remind me to find better armchairs for the office?"

"Of course. On it!," the secretary answered, typing something on his computer.

A message beeped on Hokki's phone.

Remember to order new armchair for the office.

"Perfect," he said. "Let's go get cultured."

SARAN

"Hello, you have reached the Ministry of Culture. What can I help you with?"

"Hello, I am Professor Saran Ivanova and I am the head of the scientific department of the National Museum. I would like to speak with the person in charge of the upcoming Amazon sisters' exhibit."

"A moment please."

She was put on hold to the sound of a syrupy melody and was glad she had taken those Mindfulness Helper pills.

"First Secretary Karimova," a throaty feminine voice said. "What can I help you with, Professor Ivanova?"

Saran tried to explain her query in a few words, which was difficult as she couldn't reveal the true reason behind her call.

"A moment please."

More syrupy music.

"Professor Ivanova? This is Inassa Sultanova."

Saran felt her heart jump in her throat in spite of the pills flowing in her blood. The minister of culture herself. Now she really was in the eye of the storm.

"I think you understand why I am calling, your excellency. It's about the genetic test results of the Amazon sisters."

"Yes, of course. We wrote you to keep them under wraps

until after the opening of the new wing. I thought we were clear about that."

"You were indeed, your excellency. And we will not communicate about them. But . . . what is the plan afterward?"

"You will make the results public, of course. Many people want to know."

Saran hesitated. "Aren't you worried about the consequences? I mean, our city is open to many things, but these results . . . They can lead to all sorts of political problems, if you see what I mean."

"I see very well what you mean. But we have no choice. You will have to take on the responsibility. It is also time for our country to grow up and move in a more modern direction. Princess Farah said so the other day in her speech for the opening of the International Poetry Festival."

You will have to take on the responsibility.

"Yes, of course, but . . ."

"I am counting on you. We're sisters in this, after all. And we're very lucky to have you at the museum."

The phone went dead, and Saran put it back in her pocket like a broken robot. *You will have to take on the responsibility.* The sentence ran in her head like a death sentence. In a week or so, she might land on a terrorist hit list. *Sisters my ass,* she thought. *Sisters my fucking ass.*

VITA

Back in her hotel room, Vita wasn't sure Bruno would have approved of her frontal collision method, but the Synth aura that vibrated around Thomas (if that was his real name) was one of the strongest she had experienced yet, and it gave her an advantage: he was on the run and Synth was illegal in New Samarqand too. Hell, it was illegal everywhere—the Subliminal Empire had made sure of that—and therefore he needed to keep his profile low. For the moment, Thomas probably saw her as the greatest threat of his existence. Soon, he would realize that she was his strongest ally. And maybe he would even join them in their fight against the Empire. The thought heartened her, and she picked up one of the books about UFOs she had bought in his bookstore. Weird crap, like bad sex scenes, was always entertaining.

KASSANDRA

"Did you find the books?" Naila shouted the second Kassandra walked into the apartment.

"Why are you screaming like this? I just arrived. I'm not your teenage daughter."

She puffed as she put down her bag and Naila materialized to help her take her summer jacket off.

"I am not an old woman, you know," the poetess snarled. "I am only eight years older than you."

"You could just say thank you instead of behaving like one," Naila calmly answered, hanging the jacket in the hallway.

They pucker-kissed, and Kassandra patted her lover's cheek, smiling.

"Thomas had some good books on Amazons at the English bookstore," she said, as she made her way toward their comfortable sofa in the living room. "He recommended this one, about the Greek myths, the archaeological evidence and literary references. And it's written by a woman. Perfect. Now I'm going to read it."

"Do you need anything? I have a review to finish."

"What are you reviewing?"

"An anthology of Olgeÿ Tazar."

"So it's good, then?"

"Yes, wonderful. So sad he died the way he did."

"Fanatics have always hated poetry, because they can't

understand it. Their brains are too limited and words frighten them. But they can't kill words, so they murder the poets. Can you get me a beer? A cold one? I think we have some left in the fridge."

Kassandra settled the cushions behind her back, took out her pipe and opened the book. Naila came back with the New Hellas imported beer Kassandra had her buy in a downtown super-deluxe supermarket.

"Thank you, my dear," Kassandra said, lighting her pipe.

"Anything for poetry, my dear," Naila said with a smile, before disappearing into her tiny office.

What would I do without her? Kassandra asked herself before diving into the open volume on her knees. *Oh, I know: I would lie down on the sofa with my shoes on.*

HOKKI

"There sure are a lot of jars and potteries in this wing," Hokki said, feeling his feet swell in his shoes after walking so much.

"From the Arab period to the Khwārezm-Shāh dynasty, ninth through thirteenth centuries," Jalil read out loud from the sign above the door. "That's four hundred years of pottery."

"Figures," Hokki said, feeling his stomach grumble. "Maybe we should get something to nibble and a coffee."

Jalil nodded.

On their route to the cafeteria, a troubling question suddenly popped into Hokki's mind.

"Jalil, may I ask you a stupid question?"

"You can ask me any kind of question, sir."

"Why do I need you? I mean, why have you been assigned to me?"

Jalil stopped on his tracks and stared at Hokki with both his eyebrows raised.

"Seriously, sir?"

"Yes, seriously," Hokki grunted.

"You don't know, then?"

"Know what?"

Jilal resumed walking, Hokki trotting behind.

"Know what?" he repeated.

"That Vladimir Azimov, your predecessor, was murdered.

Well, kidnapped, tortured *and* murdered, to be exact. They cut off his head with a bread knife and posted it on YouTube. Terrible thing to watch."

"They?"

"A terrorist group. We have a few of those around. Terrible people. But don't worry, I'm here to protect you. And don't forget your phone. The pink one. Easy to find!"

Hokki blanched. He had indeed read somewhere that Azimov had died "tragically." He had imagined a car accident, a bathtub electrocution while powering up his smartphone, falling from a balcony, drunk—or a suicide. But not butchered like this.

"Are you alright, sir? You look very pale. I mean, paler than usual. And you are sweating."

It was true. He didn't feel that good.

"I think I definitely need something to eat and a strong coffee. Something with a lot of sugar in it," he said.

Jalil nodded. "Food is the best defense against fear, as my mother always said."

Hokki walked faster with each passing "Cafeteria" sign—as if they were headed to the emergency ward.

ALI

So the agony of the king had been confirmed by his cousin Sekmet, high-ranking officer in the Bureau 23, someone who would never give him any information unless he expected something in return. And he did—but wouldn't get it. Not now anyway. Ali was tired of the Bureau 23 getting all the credit for "spectacular plot" discoveries that were stolen from the dedicated police masses and their informants.

Not that Bureau 23 was inefficient, far from it: but they were best in the higher spheres, the political, religious and cultural ones, where they indeed had an impressive network of informants—either willing or coerced into collaboration.

And now this: one of his officers had forwarded him a printed list that had been found near the body of Mariam Sumarova. It contained fifteen names of politicians, artists, writers and cultural personalities. Sumarova's had been crossed with a red line. No fingerprints, of course. As the list had been folded and was crumpled, it probably meant that it had fallen from someone's pocket.

Ali grabbed a file on his desk, but his eyes couldn't focus on the print and he put it back down with a sigh.

As the head of Samarqand's Egregorian Society, he could not ignore the signs. His old friend commissioner Georg Ratner from New Babylon had told him the past week that Sheryl Boncoeur, the famous TV talk-show star, had been murdered in New Babylon, probably for a political reason. The news of her death had even rippled to Samarqand where journalists voiced their concern about their own security here—which was perfectly understandable, given the circumstances. In New Belleville, there had been a terror attack against a radio station during a comedy program. And yesterday, Viborg City's government had again accused Samarqand of financing international terror groups—which was terribly ironic, given the situation. After Mariam Sumarova's murder, he was ninety-nine percent sure there would be talks of calling a state of emergency in the city. With the king in a coma and no heir officially designated, everything was in place for the perfect storm. An *égrégore* was definitely in the making here and they had to stop it before it grew too strong.

Ali knew he needed to summon an Egregorian Society meeting as soon as possible and begin working on creating the symbolic Golem that would protect the city-state. He gently slapped his cheeks, as if to wake himself up, but he knew he wasn't dreaming. The nightmare was very, very real.

SARAN

In the bus on her way home, Saran felt the half-empty tube of pills in her pocket. When she had accepted the job as head of the scientific department in the National Museum, she hadn't known it would require an addiction to the Mindfulness Helper drug. Fortunately, it was cheap and you didn't need a prescription—it was also, according to the ads, all natural and plant-based. Well, so were weed and psilocybin.

The irony was that Thomas had been an addict when she had first met him. A "Synther," as the media called them. She had tried a new cure on him in her former lab, based on a combination of an RNA-based drug and musical algorithms and, apparently, it had worked. Maybe she needed a cure too. Or another job. Or both.

She shrugged and pressed her forehead against the dirty window. The city flowed outside, unaware. She let the drug take over her mind like a mother gently rocking her sick child.

NAILA

I watch over you like a strange angel—visible, yet invisible. You see me and you love me, but there's another me hiding within. I have accepted spying on you to protect you, and that's what I am doing. But the paradox is killing me sometimes, like a powerful acid my gut would produce, eating the flesh from inside. You are so strong yourself, a block of concrete impervious to the world surrounding you, a monster of sorts sometimes and and yet—and yet, a genius, a beacon for many, as your words reach depths that few can, and give back hope when there is, in fact, none. Every night, after you have gone to bed, after we have or haven't made love, I write my report to my correspondent at Bureau 23, hoping he or she will not see through my lies. Because I am lying, every single day, for you. And, worst of all, to you.

IRIS

THOMAS

They were all sitting at a large round table in the basement of the bookstore, which you could access through another basement in a contiguous house. It made it difficult for the secret service to spot the actual entrance, or so everybody present hoped. If the Egregorian Society wasn't illegal *per se*, the regime didn't look too kindly on secret societies. What's more, its purposed power—or counter-power, to be exact—lay in its secrecy and its independence from all main political forces in the city-states where it had a chapter.

They were here, all eight of them: the cop, the bookstore manager, the doctor, the lawyer, the other lawyer, the university professor, the publisher and the psychologist. Four women and four men, as in all the society's chapters. And an even number, because it was accepted that two parts couldn't reach a consensus, as it was historically proven that the majority wasn't always right. If ever.

If the secrecy could appear childish for some, it wasn't the case for Thomas. As an exmember of a black hat hacker group, the infamous "Potemkin Crew," he knew that it could be a question of life and death. He understood it, and he cherished it. Ali cleared his voice and stood up.

"My dear friends," he said. "I have some terrible news for

you. The king is dead or at least dying. This information was confirmed to me from a trusted source yesterday."

There was a perceptible tension in the group and even if Thomas already knew the situation, he felt an unwelcome chill run down his spine.

"Is that true?" the publisher asked the doctor.

"Yes," she said. "But I can't confirm his condition either. He isn't in my service, and the nurse who told me has been moved to another unit. I don't know if that's linked to her informing me or not."

There was a quick exchange of worried commentaries until Ali signaled that he wanted to speak again.

"As you all know, this means that an *égrégore* is definitely rising, and that it will be an extremely powerful one. And we have to stop it if we can. The only advantage we have right now is that nobody knows what is really going on, except for us and a few people carefully watched by the Bureau 23. It means we can maybe attack it before it is fully blown."

"How much time do we have?" the lawyer asked.

Ali looked at the short and plump gray-haired man sitting opposite of him and shrugged.

"Well, there's the international poetry week going on, and the opening of the National Museum's new wing this weekend, so the info is not going to be leaked now. And we don't know if the king is dead or dying—which can make a big difference. But let's say, a month, max."

The university professor shook her head. "It's too late, then."

One of the lawyers, a young woman with thick glasses and tight short hair, patted the professor's wrist, shaking her head in unison.

"Maybe not quite," Ali said, attracting all the attention again. "There are at least two powerful conduits that can help us raise a Golem rather quickly. The first is Crown Princess Farah."

The psychologist made a grimace, ruining his otherwise

stunning looks. "We don't *really* know anything about her, except that she's the darling of the Western Alliance. And that she's not that popular here precisely because of this."

Ali sighed. "True, but she's also one of our best vessels. And first on the list I have here," he continued, waving a piece of paper wrapped in a police transparent zip-bag in front of his face. "It's a hit list from the Guardians of Mazda we found near Mariam Sumarova's body. We don't know if it was left there intentionally or if it has accidentally fallen out of someone's pocket. That's why we can't make the info public."

"I'm sorry to interrupt you," the professor said. "But how can she become a vessel? I thought we couldn't use politicians."

"You're right, but like a Tarot card, a vessel can have many aspects. Through her royal status, Princess Farah is also a dominant public figure. People love to read about her life in magazines, comment on her clothes, wonder what her love life is like."

"Of even if she *has* a love life," the male lawyer said, making the female lawyer giggle.

"See? That's exactly my point," Ali said, smiling. "If she gets enough radiance as a public figure, she can help build up the Golem and defeat the égrégore."

"Okay, I see what you're saying," the publisher said, waving a jeweled hand in front of her eyes. "But how are we going to gather the necessary vibrations around her?"

Ali smiled.

"We are going to tell the media she's on top of the list."

There was a moment of stunned silence.

"*We*? We can't do that. We're a secret society!" the male lawyer protested, visibly panicked.

"I mean, we'll send them a picture of the list through unidentifiable channels. Thomas knows how to do this sort of things."

"Ah, yes, okay, I see," the lawyer said, regaining his composure. "Not a bad idea. It could work."

This was the second time they had worked on creating a

protecting Golem. The first was when Thomas had arrived as a political refugee, seven years ago. That time they had used him and a poet who had just been murdered by a terrorist group, Olgeÿ Tazar. Tazar had been a national figure, and the vibes created through him, and Thomas's situation as a fugitive from the evil Western Alliance had worked wonders. The Golem had surged and destroyed the *égrégore* that had taken over the city-state, pushing it toward an ominous dictatorship. Thomas had only known later that he had been channeling these energies, but it had explained the intense autoinduced Synth dreams he had been having during that period. The cure that Saran had given him hadn't in fact stopped his Synth addiction, but had turned the Golem loose. It had been so powerful that Thomas had thought he had been cured for many years, until he realized that Synth had only been made dormant by the extreme energy release.

"A good plan indeed," the psychologist said, "but we will need a second vessel, as you all know. We could perhaps use Mariam Sumarova, but she definitely wasn't as popular as Tazar. Actually, she wasn't popular at all. Or even well-known. Her murder was only mentioned in passing in the evening news."

"Bureau 23 also didn't want to give the terrorists too much publicity, so it asked the news to keep a tight lid on the investigation," Ali explained. "But you're right. And fortunately, the second vessel is on that same list. And she's much more famous. Kassandra Alexopoulos."

The name had an impressive impact on the assembly.

"Shit!"

"Oh my God!"

"They want to kill *her*?"

Thomas was shocked. Kassandra was his friend, she had just been in his store the day before. He loved to chat with her, even if she had quite a rigid mind on some topics. He also loved her poetry, as many others did worldwide. She had just been nominated for the Clarice Lispector Award, the most prestigious literary coronation a writer could dream of. He pictured her little silhouette among his shelves, the pipe she sometimes smoked outside, and sometimes kept stuck and unlit between her teeth as she scanned the colorful paperback rows for whatever book she was looking for—yesterday, a volume on Amazons.

"Your reactions also prove my point," Ali said. "She is very popular. So you know what to do. When the info is leaked to the media, you'll have to speak about the Princess and Kassandra to as many people as possible, write columns on your page, create threads on social media and so on, so that a positive vortex can emerge. We've done it once before, we can do it again. It's our only chance, and this time, our window is very small."

Everybody agreed, even the skeptical psychologist, and the members left two at a time, waiting a few minutes between each exit, for security reasons.

Finally, only Thomas and Ali were left. The policeman handed a small USB key to Thomas.

"You know what to do," he said, before leaving in his turn.

Thomas looked at the black plastic rectangle in his hand and nodded. Indeed he did, indeed he did.

HOKKI

The party was going strong for an "impromptu" event, as Inassa, the minister of culture, had described it when she had invited him earlier today. Hokki had hesitated at first. She was his boss, and his former female employer had pressed charges against him. *Don't make the same mistake twice,* he had thought. But then again, life never repeated itself, did it? He had accepted and here he was, lost in a huge loft filled with strangers.

Jalil had gone into the kitchen to chat with the servants and had left Hokki alone in a crowd of unknown faces. What struck him most was the incredible diversity of types and costumes around him: asian, eurasian, eastern, southeastern and whatever. He was, by far, the whitest, the absolute tallest and the one with the most boring suit. Nursing his drink—a fabulous pale orange cocktail—he sat, alone, on a magnificent sofa, surrounded by yapping strangers. Inassa stood a few feet away, her back turned to him, chatting with a handsome young man in a turquoise turban. She had greeted Hokki when he had showed up and abandoned him at the bar at the other end of her immense loft overlooking the old city. Some of the guests were eyeing him, but no one had come to speak with him since his arrival. He looked at his watch and decided he would leave in half an hour.

"Are you bored?" a voice asked him from above, interrupting his thoughts.

Inassa was now standing in front of him, smiling and looking absolutely stunning.

"No, not at all," Hokki blurted, embarrassed that she had seen him peek at his watch. "I was just checking the time."

"Yes, I know the feeling. It's the same with me. So many appointments during the day. It becomes a habit."

Hokki nodded, glad she had found an explanation that suited him.

"How are you liking your new job, so far?" the minister of culture, and his immediate superior, asked him, then took a sip of her drink.

"It's fine. I'm just eager to move into my new apartment. The hotel room is nice, but one gets a little bit bored after a while. I would like to have my things around."

"Of course! I'm sorry this is taking longer than expected, but there is a shortage of workers at the moment . . . I think it's the same all over the world, or so I've heard."

"Yes, it was the same in Viborg City. It's the downfall of a good thing, I guess: poor countries are getting a little bit richer, so the people stay there."

"Yes, but we *need* them," Inassa said. "You *need* your apartment."

She bent forward to put her glass on the coffee table and a burst of the most exquisite perfume reached Hokki's nose.

"I didn't know you were so *biiig*," she suddenly said, her deep black eyes plunging into his. "You almost scare me!"

She laughed, her hand in front of her mouth.

"I'm sorry about that," Hokki answered. "Both my parents were very tall."

"They were vikings, certainly!" Inassa exclaimed. "Do you know that some vikings came to Samarqand?"

"Really?"

"Well, nobody's really sure, but there are legends. You could be one of them. So tall!"

They both laughed, Inassa sincerely and Hokki politely.

"We have to speak about the opening of the new wing, by the way. It's important. There have been some unforeseen developments . . ."

Inassa's face had morphed into the minister of culture that she was, and Hokki could almost feel the temperature drop by a couple of degrees.

"Is it delayed? Because of the foreign workers?" he asked, worried by the change of tone.

"No, more serious than that. But I can't tell you here," she whispered. "And this is not the time to talk about work! We need a new drink!"

Hokki stood up in a cloud of her perfume, and she grabbed his arm as they made their way to the bar. Her grip felt wonderful on his arm. He feared all this would come back in his dreams, later tonight—her irresistible fragrance, the softness of her fingers felt through the fabric of his jacket.

KASSANDRA

The book on Amazons she had bought at Thomas's bookstore had done wonders for her inspiration. She had gotten up early, and in her study,had typed away on her laptop for a good hour. She'd just stopped and was contemplating the beginning of her poem with satisfaction when Naila walked in, phone in hand.

"Oh, sorry, I didn't know you were working."

"I'm always working, my dear."

"Even when you're napping."

"Especially when I'm napping. What did you want?"

"Your phone rang. You left it in the dining room. I took the call and it's a policeman. He wants to talk to you."

"A policeman? Why? Did you kill somebody?"

"No. Did you?"

"Not recently, no. Give me that phone . . . Allo?"

"Hello, this is Commissioner-General Ali Shakr Bassam speaking. I am sorry to disturb you, but this is very important."

"Yes?"

"I don't really know how to tell you this, but your name has appeared on a hit list left behind by a terrorist group. You might be in great danger."

"Oh!"

"Yes. I'm sorry."

"It's not your fault."

"No, well, I mean . . . Anyway . . . you will have some police protection from now on. A police officer will be assigned to you and will protect you until this group is neutralized."

"Is that really necessary?"

"I'm afraid so."

"But I have to work on this poem for the opening of the museum this weekend. I can't entertain a guest. And I smoke a pipe."

"She will be very discreet, I promise."

"I can't say no, I guess."

"No. She will be at your door in about half an hour. Her name is Aisha."

"Wait a minute! How do I know you're not a terrorist yourself? This could be a trap."

She heard the man sigh at the other end.

"Indeed, it could be. Well thought. But we can Skype if you want. You'll see me in my office."

"I was joking. But no matter. I'll wait for her. And thank you."

Naila was anxious to hear what the cop had told her.

"I am more famous than I imagined," Kassandra said. "And, apparently, some people really, really hate my poetry."

SARAN

Thomas was still sleeping, but Saran lay awake, staring at the ceiling. She had just killed her phone alarm, and it was the first time in all these years that she didn't feel like going to work. She now remembered that when she had gotten the position, Thomas had congratulated her, but also warned her about its political implications. "Everything is political here. They need to show the Western Alliance that they're moving in the right direction and they're naming women to all sorts of responsibilities. It's a front. And you might become a hostage in something much bigger than yourself. I know because that's exactly what happened to me. I am free and protected here because I serve New Samarqand's interests. When that's over, I might have to flee again. And you're exactly in the reverse position. As long as we move closer to the Western Alliance, your position is safe. But if things get suddenly cooler . . . You're gone."

She cuddled up against him and caressed his blond stubble. Their relationship was built on a paradox—Thomas the eternal rebel, she the model citizen. They still loved each other—or at least, she thought so—but they seemed to be slowly drifting apart. There wasn't any jealousy, any real fight, any reproach, and yet she felt as if their partnership was becoming more and more dematerialized. Like ghosts, they talked and shared their daily info, their hopes and occasional fears, but the physical was almost gone. The few times they made love, it felt like it was in accelerated time, as if they had just remembered that their bodies existed.

Thomas grunted and opened his eyes.

"What time is it?" he asked.

She told him and he frowned, his handsome features still blurred by sleep.

"Aren't you going to be late for work? You're usually already out the door by this time. "

She cuddled up against him, her cheek feeling the warmth of his chest. If she listened closely, she could hear his heart beat. His hand landed in her hair like a heavy bird making its nest.

"I think I'm going to stay home today," she said. "I don't feel like going to work. I'll call in sick."

"What's wrong, darling? Bad vibes at work?"

She shrugged and sighed. "Yes. Very. I think I might lose my job, to be honest."

She felt her chin wobble and warm tears bathe the bottom of her eyes. *Just like in a fucking anime*, she thought as she felt her cheeks get wet. Thomas hugged her tighter and kissed the top of her head.

"Why would they fire you, baby? You're the bestest! Hell, you even cured me!"

She took a deep breath, wiped her tears with her palm and explained the situation as clearly as possible. Thomas remained silent for a while, and she wondered with some irritation if he had fallen asleep again.

"Wait a minute," he finally said. "If the Amazon sisters are not genetically related, as the tests seem to prove, then they must have been . . . lovers?"

"Most probably, yes," Saran said feebly. "You can imagine the scandal it will make here . . . And the minister of culture clearly told me it was going to be my problem. I'd better look for another job now."

Thomas grunted, which meant he agreed.

"You could start an illegal Synth lab," he said. "You're a biochemist, after all."

She slapped him hard on the chest. "That's not funny!" she protested.

But it was. And she smiled. And it made her feel a little better.

ALI

The young cop in uniform walked into his office without knocking, saluted and dropped the pile of the morning newspapers on his desk. The commissioner-general absentmindedly picked up the first one on the pile. He enjoyed this routine, which provided him both with ordinary news and secondhand Intel: the choice of headlines and stories featured (or not featured) always gave him a hint on local politics, which was crucial in his position. He saw with some relief that the King's condition was reported as stable, and his eyes zigzagged over the various foreign politics reports. He saw with satisfaction that Thomas had leaked the info about Princess Farah being on the terrorists' hit list. *That will give our Golem some good energy*, he thought. Then he turned the page and felt with panic that the *égrégore* had grown even bigger and stronger overnight.

He took out his personal phone and dialed Sekmet's number.

"I was about to call you," his cousin said on the other end.

HOKKI

Hokki lay in the most comfortable bed he had ever fucked in. His head was nested between Inassa's large and beautiful breasts, bobbing slowly up and down as she breathed, like a raft on the open sea. *You did it again, you fool,* he thought. *You did it again.*

Inassa's perfume surrounded him like a heavenly mist, mixing with the more common and familiar smells of sex. He wondered what time it was, although it didn't really matter if he was late for work, as he was in bed with his boss. *Again.*

He wondered what Jalil, who had been sent to one of the numerous guest rooms, would think of the whole situation. Maybe he would tell Hokki that he should have used his pink phone and called for help. Well, to be perfectly honest, he was glad he hadn't. An unforgettable night of pure orgasmic bliss.

"So, tell me, my dear, why is there an arrest warrant hanging over your head in Viborg City?"

Inassa had whispered, but her words resounded like unexpected thunder in Hokki's ears.

So she knew. Damn. Damn. Damn.

Hokki had been aware that she would eventually find out, but not that fast. Their secret police was alarmingly efficient. He cleared his throat while carefully planning his words.

"It's complicated," he explained, purposely lingering on the words. Slow was always more convincing. "I had this girlfriend who was a very powerful woman in Viborg City. A minister, like you. She had gotten me the position as director for the city's modern art museum."

"Oh, oh! Corruption in Viborg City? The 'Moral Compass' of the Western Alliance? Who would have thought?" Inassa interrupted in mock surprise.

Hokki smiled and shrugged.

"Well . . . Yes. It can definitely be seen that way, I admit. Anyway, things got sour between us when she found out I was seeing somebody else on the side."

"Seeing, like 'fucking'?"

"Yes."

"Not good."

"No, not good."

"You're a bad man."

"I *was* a bad man. I learned my lesson," Hokki defended himself.

"Maybe I should deliver you immediately to Viborg City. Female solidarity, you know."

Hokki felt a cold wind of panic blow though his body.

"I swear to you I've changed! That woman, that minister, Karin, she was a bad woman. A true narcissist and very mean to her employees. Hell, she directly fired more than eight people during my term!"

"Well, we have known each other for a little more than a week and I already fired two . . ."

"I'm sure they deserved it."

"They certainly did. And she pressed charges against you just because you were unfaithful?"

Hokki grunted and shook his head, feeling her wonderful skin press against his cheeks.

"No. She got me fired and said it was because I had misused public funds."

"Oh. And have you?"

"No. I mean, not really. She let me use her professional credit card a couple of times, and later she claimed I had done it behind her back. I didn't even use it that much."

"It says in the warrant that you bought a sports car, a trip to some exotic island and even an apartment."

"It was a very small one and Viborg City is incredibly expensive. And all those were gifts from Karin. I swear!"

Hokki felt Inassa's finely manicured nail glide against the stubble of his cheek and thought of a steel blade.

"With this warrant over your head, you are my thing now," she said, kissing his hair. "My adorable giant sexy plaything. You will be closely watched, and if you fuck up, I can assure you that Viborg City's prison will seem like an unattainable paradise to you. Understood?"

Hokki nodded. "Understood," he answered.

"Good. Now let's fuck again. You need to enjoy your freedom while it lasts."

THOMAS

Thomas opened the shop and walked into the familiar and dusty labyrinth of wood, cardboard and paper. Sometimes he was surprised that objects such as books still existed in this more and more virtual world: vulnerable, decaying, cumbersome. But humans had adapted around them, confirming both the Darwinian rule of evolution and a Taoist truth: the fittest for survival wasn't always the most directly useful.

Saran had finally gone to work after breakfast, late for the first time in the six years she had worked at the museum's lab. She probably felt her responsibilities were too important even if she now knew the whole thing had been a clever trap. Her dedication to her work and to her city-state government had often made him cringe, and had led to sometimes violent arguments—always verbal, never physical—but he deeply loved her and wished he could support her more. As a political refugee, he was split between his gratefulness for the city's protection and his aversion for any authoritarian regime. He sat down behind his desk in his little office and took his personal laptop out of his backpack.

There was one coded message from New Tokyo. He switched to the dark net and opened his mailbox. It was a delivery for the vault: all classic Japanese films from 1897 to the early 2000s. The vault was one of the reasons Thomas was glad he had joined the Egregorian Society. It was a project to protect all of Earth's culture from economic and political destruction—films, books, comic-strips, music, art. Everything was illegally stored on the Egregorian Society's massive servers. Whenever a classic became unavailable through the official commercial channels, the Egregorian Society would feed it back to pirate sites for free access, making sure that these works would survive in the collective memory. Thomas didn't know exactly how many Egregorian Society cells there were in the world—secrecy meant safety—but they all had access to the vault, and he liked to imagine the virtual treasures buried there. He checked his New Tokyo contact identity and clicked on the download link. In a few hours, more precious objects would be added to the loot, forever protected by the Society.

He walked back into the shop to price a new pile of books. The tedious routine of the capitalist market.

KASSANDRA

"And you are?"

"Sergeant Aisha Alieva. Commissioner-General Ali Shakr Bassam sent me. I am here for your protection."

Kassandra scrutinized the young woman in uniform from head to toe with a critical eye, then opened the door, Naila peeking over her left shoulder.

"Nice to meet you, sort of," the poet added as the policewoman stepped in. "This is Naila, my secretary. You can talk to her. I have to work."

"Would you like some tea?" Naila asked the cop. "I've just made some."

Kassandra closed the door of her study before hearing the answer. *Well, at least, Naila will have someone to complain to about me,* she thought as she sat down in front of her laptop and lit her pipe. *She will probably remember these events as the best times of her life.*

SARAN

Saran was on the bus trying to make up an excuse for being late to work when her mobile phone rang. It was her top boss, the minister of culture. Frowning, she slid her thumb toward the green symbol.

"Have you seen the news?" the minister said, without even identifying herself.

"No. What news?"

"It's on all the news media. Check them out and call me back when you're in your office. Alone."

Fearing the worst, Saran opened the browser on her phone and clicked the main newspaper's link. It was right under the headlines, obvious enough. You didn't even have to scroll down.

DNA tests shows that Amazon "sisters" were not related.

Her hand automatically searched for her Mindfulness Pills and, this time, she swallowed two instead of the recommended one.

ALI

"We probably need to place this woman under maximum protection too," Ali told his cousin from Bureau 23, who was sitting on the other side of his desk.

Given the circumstances, they had decided it was safer to talk in person in Ali's office. They were now watching the news channel on the muted flat-screen TV hanging on his wall, and they could see Saran run into the building, surrounded by journalists.

"Actually, we're already monitoring her," Sekmet said. "Have been for a while."

"Because of her partner? The Viborg City exhacker turned bookseller?"

"Yes. Your friend."

Ali felt a slight chill, but he already knew that Bureau 23 had a tag on Thomas. And on him. Especially on him.

"Any news about the king?" the commissioner-general asked, to deflect the conversation.

"None that I can give you," Sekmet said. "But let's say it hasn't improved."

"This is one crazy week," Ali said.

"It's only Tuesday today," Sekmet reminded him.

"Oh yes," Ali said. "I forgot."

"We need to collaborate more closely," Sekmet said. "Maybe you should give me the list of your informants, so we can cross-check them. Some might be members of the Guardians of Mazda, without you knowing it."

"Yes, maybe," Ali nodded, scratching his chin at the same time.

Bad idea, he thought. *Very bad idea. This is not about safety, this is about politics. About controlling information and potential damage when the king's death is announced.*

"I will send you the list," he said without saying when. "But for now, what do we do?"

Sekmet sighed. "We wait, crossing our fingers that the whole thing doesn't blow up. The prime minister will probably tell the media to tone down their articles about the Amazon dykes and promote the international poetry festival more. That's what I would do, in any case. In the meantime, I would suggest maximum security for the opening of the new wing. And tell your people to keep a good eye on the new museum director too. We don't want to lose him like we lost his predecessor."

VITA

Vita parked her motorbike in front of the bookstore. She wanted to sell back her UFO books (which sucked) and take the opportunity to chat with Thomas about their possible alliance, and an introduction to that poet she was supposed to protect, Kassandra Alexopoulos. She had been surfing the net to find more info and all the news she could find online about New Samarqand—there were two newspapers with an English edition—and she now understood why Bruno wanted her here. This place was perfect for the Subliminal Empire: a dangerous mix of geopolitical tensions and local instabilities. Very rich—rare minerals and the largest solar energy farm in the world—but too small to lead its international politics independently. The king seems to have tired of the classic alliance with the Chinese Confederation and had slowly moved toward the Western Alliance. It wasn't clear yet what the city-state would win with this shift, but it sure fueled local debates, and even violence. From what she had understood, there were terrorist groups—probably manipulated by the Chinese Confederation, but who knew?—who wanted a strict religious regime, while students had violently demonstrated a few months ago for a less patriarchal society. Of course, all of this was closely observed with great interest by the Western Alliance and its media, fueling heated discussions there too. Such a crisis was a blessing for the Subliminal Empire, as its final goal was pure political and cultural entropy, which was easier achieved through well-manipulated chaos. Her own Planet X and many others before it had fallen to such a ploy.

Vita had no idea what part this poetess Bruno had told her to protect played in all this, but she must have an incredible importance in this interplanetary game. Vita had read all she could about her: Kassandra Alexopoulos originally came from New Athens, but had come to New Samarqand after the civil war had ravaged her city-state. She was a world-famous poet, known for the beauty of her verses but also her staunch political themes: feminism, environment and human rights. In spite of the rather conservative Samarqandi society, she had been adopted by her new home and had won numerous national and international prizes. She had just been short-listed for the Clarica Lispector Award, which was the most prestigious literary distinction today. *Quite a woman*, Vita had thought. *Or rather: quite* the *woman.*

She pulled the bookstore's dirty glass door open and bumped into a police officer. She apologized and the woman in uniform asked to see her bag. Vita mentally thanked herself not to have brought her gun with her. The police woman thoroughly checked her backpack, pulling out the books one by one and carefully feeling the bottom with her hand before finally letting her walk in.

"Sorry about that," said a small feminine figure standing next to Thomas on the other side of the shop. "She won't leave me alone for a minute. I'm afraid I will lose many of my friends now."

Vita approached the silhouettes, and Kassandra smiled, extending her hand.

"Kassandra Alexopoulos, dangerous poet."

"Vita. Just passing through. Honored to meet you. You're very famous."

Kassandra grunted. "Have you read any of my poetry?" she asked, her black eyes sparkling with amusement.

"No, I must admit I haven't. Yet."

"Then I'm not *that* famous. Thomas, do you have any of my books here? Get one for Vita. Put it on my tab."

Thomas graciously did as he was told, and Vita heard him rummage in one of the parallel shelves. He quickly came back with a book which he was about to hand to Vita, when Kassandra grabbed it.

"The cover is dog-eared," she said, examining it. "And so are some pages. Don't you have other copies?"

Thomas shook his head, smiling. *He looks used to the poetess's antics*, Vita analyzed. *Old friends indeed.*

"*It's fine*," Vita said. "Thank you."

"Let me sign it first," the poetess said, finding a pen in her handbag. "You can sell it for a good price on the net if you ever need some money."

"Thank you. I'll think about that."

"I like her," Kassandra said, turning to Thomas. "Do you know her?"

"We've met once before," Thomas said. "We come from the same city."

"And we have common friends," Vita added.

"Really? I would love to hear more of your stories. Who comes to visit New Samarqand these days, *n'est-ce pas*? Would you like to come over and have some tea? I live right around the corner."

"I would be honored, thank you."

Kassandra hooked her arm in Vita's and blew a kiss in Thomas's direction.

"*Au revoir, mon ami.* Do not despair, I'll come back soon!"

As they walked onto the sun-splashed noisy morning street followed by the silent female cop, Vita thought she had finally met an interesting person on this planet.

HOKKI

In the car, Hokki was very confused. Everything had happened in a flash, although he didn't really know what this "everything" was about. He had just walked out of Inassa's building when Jalil had received a phone call. The security officer had chatted briefly in Samarqandi, looking more and more somber, nodding sharply once in a while. Hokki's first thoughts were that either his affair with his boss had already been disclosed to the media, or that she was sending him back to Viborg City on the first plane. Or both.

"In the car, hurry," Jalil had said.

"Where are we going?" Hokki had asked as Jalil drove away.

"I don't know yet. I'm waiting for my orders."

"Orders? What orders?"

"You have the pink phone, yes?"

"Yes, yes. It's in my pocket. At all times, as you said. See?"

"Good. Don't answer your other phone. Just this one."

"Jalil, what's going on?"

"Sorry, I can't tell you now."

"Am I in danger?"

"It's a possibility."

Jalil's phone rang again and a short conversation ensued.

"What was that about?" Hokki asked.

"Your new address. I'm driving you there now."

"My new address? You mean, my new apartment, right? Why all the fuss?"

Jalil just shrugged, concentrating on the traffic and Hokki's mind ran wild in all possible directions.

SARAN

The nightmare had begun earlier than she had expected, but thanks to the Mindfulness Helper pills, everything seemed to crash around her in slow motion. She had tried to contact her minister, then the museum director—the new one, with a foreign name, Hokki something—but to no avail. Her office phone kept ringing and emails from journalists were piling up in her computer. She remembered Thomas's words about her being the "useful idiot" and felt angry at the truth they contained.

Someone had leaked the DNA results to the press. Someone had done it with the direct purpose of ruining her career, and at the possible cost of civil peace. Someone who despised her and wanted her position. Even though she could name a few suspects, one seemed the most probable: Akmet.

Her mobile phone rang. It was the culture minister. Finally.

"So the cat is out of the bag," Inassa said.

"Yes. I'm sorry."

"Not your fault, I presume. But an unexpected nuisance, nonetheless."

"I tried to contact the new director, but he doesn't pick up my calls."

"He's in trouble too, and it's not his fault either. Hell, the poor man just arrived . . . Anyway, he was told not to answer his phone. My orders."

"I guess you want my resignation. I will send it to you right after this conversation. I understand perfectly. I haven't been cautious enough."

"No, I don't. Not yet anyway. I've booked you an interview with Channel One in an hour, in your office. And you're going to say exactly what I'm going to tell you right now. You're going to take full responsibility for the leakage. You're going to tell them you've done it."

"What? But . . . but—"

"Don't interrupt me. You're going to say you did it against the will of my ministry, because you're a modern woman and you think this city has to move forward. And then you'll say you resign."

So the ax is falling in order to protect the powerful, Saran thought. "Okay," she said feebly. "I understand."

"No you don't. I'm not finished. Akmet Lebedev will replace you. I will promote him this evening."

Saran felt the walls of her office sway as if a psychic earthquake had hit the building.

"Yes," she managed to say, although her mouth was suddenly dry. "It makes sense."

"It does," Inassa resumed. "He leaked the results. We traced the source without any problem. He's obviously an amateur when it comes to these things."

Saran frowned, her despair slowly being replaced by a cold anger.

"And that's why you're promoting him?"

"Yes. To protect you."

"What? How?" Saran stuttered, her anger melting into confusion.

"It's very simple: he will have to deal with the shit storm, which is right now above anybody's strength. And he will fail. And you can come back then."

"I really don't understand."

"No, you can't."

Saran heard her minister take a deep breath.

"Listen, let's say there are a lot of things going on at the moment in the political backstage. This plan is not one hundred percent fail-proof, I must tell you. But right now that's the best we can do for the future. You will understand when the time comes. I am behind you, I promise. You are precious to us. Much more than you might realize."

Saran remained silent, not knowing what to say. She was thinking of Akmet, that she had been right and that he would love to see her go. She also realized that it would go as Inassa had told her: that he would fail miserably.

"Okay," she finally said.

"Excellent! I knew we could count on you. I will contact you later. And don't worry—you'll get your job back. I promise."

As Saran put her mobile phone back on her desk, Thomas materialized in her thoughts. He had been right: everything was political in this city-state. Everything. She had been so naïve . . . Maybe she should become more like Thomas, sarcastic and rebellious. She understood better why he had been addicted to Synth for so long. The only way to survive mentally had been to psychically manipulate the world around him. But she was different. She wanted to belong, she wanted to be part of this society. The idea that she had to resign from her somewhat prestigious position was a deep blow for her. She felt betrayed, she felt used and abused by the system. And yet, deep down in herself, she knew she had to cope. If Thomas was all about revolt, she was all about coping. Her hand searched in her pocket for a Mindfulness Helper pill.

KASSANDRA

Talk about a "mysterious stranger" . . . The girl was simply incredible. She couldn't believe her luck to have met her. Vita. What a name, so full of poetic possibilities. And her story—*oh, mon Dieu*. Was she really a rogue agent from the Viborg City secret service? And on a mission to protect her, Kassandra Alexopoulos, the little poetess from New Athens, because some people didn't like her poetry?

"You're not little. You're world famous. And on the Clarice Lispector Award short list," Naila said, pouring some more tea into Kassandra's glass. "And the girl is surely crazy. Nice and convincing, but crazy."

"I love it," Kassandra said. "And I want to try these pills she gave us."

"Are you nuts? They might be poison! And they're surely illegal! Remember that you have a cop standing in front of our door 24/7—and that some people want you dead in this city!"

Kassandra shrugged and crossed her legs in her armchair. "Why would she want to kill me? We just met."

Naila sighed. "Oh, you are so impossible sometimes! Give me those pills. I'll flush them."

Kassandra shook her head. "No. I am interested. I took some LSD when I was in my twenties. I liked it."

Naila frowned. "Always the rebel. One day, it will kill you," she said, then immediately brought her hand over her mouth. "I'm sorry, I didn't mean it like that . . . It's because I love you so much, but you can be so irritating."

Kassandra smiled and took her companion's hands into hers.

"Darling, the role of a poet is, precisely, to be irritating. And now, *mon coeur*, I need to get some inspiration for that poem."

She grabbed the morning paper Naila had left unfolded on the coffee table and her eyes stopped midpage.

"You don't say," she whispered. "You don't say . . ."

"What?" Naila asked.

"The Amazon sisters, they weren't sisters after all . . . They were dykes, like us."

"Don't use that word!" Naila protested.

"Now I can write my poem!" Kassandra exclaimed, standing up. "Fuck that family bullshit, let's go for a real queer love hymn!"

"Remember homosexuality is a crime in this city!" Naila yelped as Kassandra slammed the study door behind her.

HOKKI

"What is this place?" Hokki asked, embracing the huge loft with his eyes. "Is it my new apartment?"

"No, sir. Just a temporary one. All the windows have bullet-proof glass, and only you and I can use the elevator to this floor. I will give you the code. The entrance door and the door to your room are bullet and fireproof too. And there are some gas masks in the dresser over there."

"Can you tell me what's going on now?"

"Wait a minute," Jalil said, and he walked to a laptop sitting on a table. He turned it on, tapped something on the keyboard, waited for a few seconds than said something in Samarqandi. A familiar voice answered him. Inassa. Had she kidnapped him to use him as a private toy-boy? he wondered. Jalil signaled Hokki to come to the laptop.

"Hello, my dear," his boss and new lover said on the screen. "Very sorry for the inconvenience. Unfortunately, it might be necessary for a few days. Or weeks. Who knows?"

She laughed, but Hokki didn't.

"Have you just kidnapped me?"

"What? No, no, my dear, we're just protecting you. The Samarqandi government is protecting you, to be exact."

"Why? What happened?"

"Some DNA results about the two Amazon sisters were leaked to the press . . . They weren't sisters, which is very unfortunate."

"I don't understand."

"We are quite a conservative country, Hokki. The idea of having two lovers of the same sex in a museum is almost a blasphemy for many people here. An insult to their religion and education. Plus we have to change the name of the wing now. It can't be called 'The Amazon Sisters' Wing' anymore."

"What does it have to do with me, precisely?"

"Well, there are some violent groups . . . like the Guardians of Mazda, for instance. They like to kill people who don't see things as they do. You are the director of the museum, therefore you are in danger, and we have to protect you. Is everything clearer now?"

Hokki nodded, still full of doubt, nonetheless.

"What about my clothes? My stuff?"

"Someone will deliver it later, don't worry. And thank you for attending my party yesterday. It was . . . divine to have you."

The screen turned black, and Hokki muttered some insults in Finnish.

"The pink phone—" Jalil began.

"I know, I know," Hokki mumbled walking towards the fridge. He hoped it would be stacked with alcohol.

THOMAS

Thomas tried to sort the books crowding his desk, but his thoughts kept drifting to Saran, who had just called him. She was in a panic, and he could totally sympathize. To realize that you're only a pawn in a huge political chess-game is the hardest reality-check ever. Hell, he knew all about that. Tried to swipe the pieces off the chessboard in Viborg City and got himself swiped instead, directly in the city's high-security jail. He wondered what he could tell Saran this evening, when he got home. They had somewhat drifted apart the past year, for reasons he couldn't really understand. That's why the Synth had kicked back into his life, probably. A way to compensate for the feeling of loneliness that sometimes seeped into his heart. Maybe this episode would pull them closer—at least, he hoped so. He let Synth irrigate his brain and turn the shop into a 1980s modernist boutique with flashy colors and lots of transparent glass tables.

The bell jingled as the door opened and that Vita woman walked in again.

"Hi," she said. "Do you buy back books you sell?"

"No, but I told you last time that you could exchange them for new ones, for a very low price. And you said it was a bad business plan."

She smiled.

"True. I remember now. Anyway, here you are. To be honest, they suck."

Thomas looked at the three volumes she had added to the pile.

"Books on UFOs generally suck, yeah," he said.

Vita shrugged. "I'll know next time. Nice shop you've arranged," she added, looking around. "Love the setup and the colors. You're good with your Synth."

"Thanks," Thomas said, feeling uneasy.

"I think we should resume our talk about that possible . . . alliance. This city-state is falling to pieces, and we can't let that happen. We both have our reasons: you're a fugitive, and you don't want to have to run away again. Plus, where would you go? The Chinese Confederation and the Eastern Alliance would not welcome a top-notch hacker known for blowing up military satellites, even if they were Western Alliance ones. Especially a hacker with your political color—you would end up in their prisons very quickly. Anarchism in totalitarian societies usually gets you there. Or simply killed. They can do that."

Thomas nodded slowly. "I'm listening," he said. "But I don't trust you. Just so you know."

"And why would you? Let me just show you something."

The 80s boutique suddenly transformed into a Viborg City secret service office.

"Recognize this? This is the building where they interrogated you, and this is my office. My old office, I mean. Today, another agent is sitting in my chair, probably trying to find my trail."

"Why did you escape?"

Vita sighed, her dark eyes sinking deep into his. "I volunteered for a secret experiment, based on drugs. They were trying to find the ultimate truth serum. Somehow, they'd gotten some Synth and they gave it to me. That's how I realized I came from another planet, and that the Subliminal Empire was trying to take over the Earth as it had with other worlds. All my memories came back. And that's when I connected with Dr. Sojo and later with Bruno. All are refugees from Planet X, like me."

Thomas shook his head. "I understand now why you think these UFO books are crap. Jesus!"

"We don't have much time," Vita said. "You don't have to believe me, but you've got to help me."

"The Subliminal Empire? Seriously?"

Vita nodded with a stern face. "I know I sound crazy, but I swear to you that I'm completely sane. Don't you feel yourself that things have been changing, for the past twenty years or so? That all the shops are beginning to be the same, that there is almost no point in traveling to other countries anymore, as you will find identical franchises and products on all the main avenues and boulevards? That music is becoming frighteningly monotonous, formatted, bland—and the same with all forms of art and culture?"

"I would agree on the music," Thomas said.

"That's how the Empire works. Getting all their power and energy out of conformity and obedience. They never use direct violence—it's much worse: they use *us*, feed us with what we imagine we want most in order to "belong." Their empire is all about influence through voluntary brainwashing. And Synth is the only weapon that works against it."

"Synth? A weapon?"

"Yes. Like a handmade explosive to sabotage train tracks. Except the train tracks are in your own brain."

"How?"

"Synth frees you from the Subliminal Empire's pseudoreality. It makes you decide which reality you want to live in, without directly causing you any harm. It's the ultimate weapon."

"I can see that," Thomas admitted. "That's exactly how I use it."

"I know. We're on the same wavelength. Literally."

They both laughed, Thomas uneasily.

"Let's say I believe you. Or somewhat believe you. What do you want from me?"

Vita let her head drop at an angle, looking intensely at Thomas.

"We would like to ally ourselves with the Egregorian Society. We believe we share the same goals, if not for the same reasons. We can help the Society too, by giving you info, for instance. Or direct support, if needed."

"Whoa, wait a minute! How do you know about all this? How do I know you're not setting me up? I've been through shit like this before!"

The door of the Vita's Viborg City office suddenly opened and an elegant young man walked in, dressed in a dark overcoat and shiny laced-up leather shoes. He wore a set of white earpods and the bluest gaze one had ever seen.

"My name is Bruno," the young man said. "I work with Vita. You don't know me, but I know you. A little, at least. Turn off the Synth for a second, and then turn it back on. Go on."

Thomas complied, dumbfounded. He switched off the Synth and was back in the bookstore, with Vita. No Bruno. He switched the drug back in his brain. Bruno smiled.

"You have to believe us. And work with us. We can connect your organization with many artists and writers around the world who need your help. With Synth and the Egregorians, we can limit the Empire's grip and make this world . . . more livable. At least for a while, if humans don't fuck things up— which is a high probability. But we need to believe it's possible, because otherwise this planet is finished, and Vita and I will have to move on."

Bruno's voice was both seductive and convincing. Synth was good to help you detect bullshit, generally. In fact, it always blocked bullshit, turning it into incomprehensible garbage. Thomas could hear every word very clearly.

"Okay," he finally said. "I will work with you, but in the beginning, I won't tell the others. You'll reach the Egregorian

Society through me, and only me. Then later, if I'm convinced of your intentions, I'll put you in contact with the others."

"Deal. Vita will be your contact. You guys are going to do a great job together," Bruno said before dematerializing in a haze of tiny lightning-like flashes.

"Wow," Thomas said. "This is . . . intense."

Vita extended her hand, which he shook. It was warm and strong. *A good hand*, he thought. *Even though the girl might be batshit crazy.*

NAILA

You said that you loved me today. Not directly, of course, but you called me "darling" and "*mon coeur.*" And here I am, writing my daily report to the authorities, as if I was heartless. I have to tell them about the visit of that strange girl, but I will just call her a "lunatic" and say that she was a foreign fan of yours, visiting our beautiful city-state as a tourist. No need to worry about her, she was harmless, I think. No foreign power would send someone with such a crazy story on a mission. And this story about this drug that could free you from oppression . . . As if! But of course, *you* loved it. I could see it in your eyes. You drank in every word she said. And she was pretty, I admit. Rough looking, but her face had nice features and her eyes were almost as intense as yours. Maybe even more intense. But not in a good way, like yours. I am sure she will inspire you and that I will recognize her in your poems. You do that often. It is fortunate I am not the jealous type. I will finish my report saying that you told me she was fun to chat with, and I'll leave it at that. "Vita." A crazy name too, if you want my opinion. Which you never do. But here it is nonetheless.

VITA

Sitting on her hotel room bed, Vita checked her stuff. The invisibility cape was charged up, and her hyperkinetic gun was ready to use if necessary. Her mission was under control: Bruno's intervention seemed to have convinced Thomas to help them, and now she knew where the poetess lived. She had set up a few small cameras in the rooms she had been in and had left Kassandra a small bag of Synth pills. Poets were usually curious, and she would make an excellent recruit. The Subliminal Empire could never break such a personality. She now understood what Bruno saw in her—and she agreed. The cameras were set so they would warn her if any intruder walked into Kassandra's apartment. She wasn't going to spy on her, just protect her.

Thomas had also provided her with some useful information about the political situation in New Samarqand, the king was pushing slightly toward the Western alliance but meeting resistance from his own followers. To make things even more complicated, his son, Prince Hamad, had criticized his father's decisions and reforms, while Princess Farah had voiced her support for this course. The kids were twins, and no one knew who their father— who apparently was sick and lay in a hospital—would choose as his royal heir. In her conversation with Kassandra, the poetess seemed to like the princess more, which was understandable, although she also said that if Princess Farah reigned, it would lead to more political turmoil. Vita had therefore understood the importance of the tiny kingdom from the Subliminal Empire's perspective: chaos always led to imposed order, no matter which kind of order. More turmoil, more bad vibes, more possibilities of chaos and, ultimately, entropy and control.

Vita put her stuff back in her backpack and took out the book Kassandra had given her. It was called *The Sum of All Things.* A poetry collection. Of course. She read the first poem, which she liked. It was short and to the point, not too obscure, nor too obvious. Settling with her back against the pillow, she turned the pages slowly, enjoying all the words describing the world as it was and always should be.

DIAMOND

ALI

Ali had been on the phone with Sekmet all morning. The opening of the new wing of the National Museum was in a couple of hours but he felt like it was only a few seconds away.

The last few days had been horribly trying. The Amazon sisters' DNA revelation had made it to the foreign media, bringing a much unwanted spotlight on the local situation. Predictably, the Western Alliance news agencies stressed the conservative reaction of the Samarqandi public and political figures, appealing for more openness. Princess Farah had expressed her opinion that it was time for Samarqand to evolve toward a more progressive society. If the inspector agreed deep down inside, he thought it premature for the princess to take such a stand, and dangerous politically. In the following hour, Prince Hamad had taken the side of the conservative wing, defending national values and traditions.

"Here we go," Ali told his wife as they watched the news. "Chaos unleashed."

"You always exaggerate everything," she answered, gently tapping his thigh. "I hope this will prove to the people how stupid he really is, and that we need a queen."

The government had tried to shift the focus of the national media on the International Poetry Week, which had been a great local success, but to no avail. The Amazons were stealing the show.

Ali had never talked so much with Sekmet, who was also

worried. The leak on the Amazons' DNA meant that the same could happen about the king's health. There were reassuring bulletins passed on to the press every day by Bureau 23 officials, but the worst could always come. If a member of the Guardians of Mazda or any other terrorist organization had infiltrated the hospital crew, there could be uncontrollable damage.

To make things worse—for him, at least—the poetess Kassandra Alexopoulos had won the prestigious Clarice Lispector Award, turning her into the perfect target for terrorists. And being the stubborn mule that she was, she had rejected extra protection, claiming that she was "shielded by the invisible angel of poetry, more powerful than his laughable police force." Apparently, success had turned her into a lunatic. His only hope now was that the Egregorians had managed to gather all the energy necessary for the manifestation of the protective Golem, should one be needed.

"So, is everything set for the ceremony?" Sekmet asked, popping the commissioner's worry-bubble.

"Yes. The security officers are already there, and we've checked the place twice for bombs. What about you?"

"We have our agents there too, among the guests and officials. Let's keep our fingers crossed. Both the prince and the princess are attending. We can't let a tragedy happen."

"No, indeed," Ali agreed. "Glad to have you with us"

"Me too, cousin," Sekmet answered to Ali's big surprise.

Sekmet had never given him anything close to a compliment before. This stressed the gravity of the situation. They ended their conversation, and Ali looked at his watch. He had been invited to attend to the opening in his capacity of head of the Samarqandi police. Although he hated these kind of events, he had to go. He called one of the on duty cops working the big desk in the hall, and told him to drive him there. At least, he wouldn't have to deal with the traffic himself.

VITA

Vita was right behind Kassandra and Naila, hidden under her invisibility cape. She had shown Kassandra how it worked on her second visit, and the poetess had been impressed. "This is wonderful, my dear," she had said. "You are like a goddess of Antiquity! Appearing and disappearing at will!"

Vita had asked Naila to leave the room for the demonstration, as this had to remain as secret as possible. It wasn't very nice of her, she knew, but there was no need to run additional risk if it could be avoided. "Never trust anyone" was the only rule she abided by. And until now, she had been proven right.

They had exited the taxi and were now walking toward the entrance of the huge building. There was a lot of security, and they had to wait in line for a few minutes before entering. Once inside, she followed the two women until they arrived in the reception hall of the new wing of the museum, which was, indeed, magnificent. There, she carefully climbed onto the pedestal of a huge statue of some kind of Chinese-style demon, from which she could observe the whole space. There were eight rows of chairs and a small stage with a microphone. She saw Kassandra take a seat in the front row, and Naila behind her. Riot-uniform-clad police officers stood all around the room, with automatic weapons and gasmasks hanging over their bulletproof protected chests.

What can go wrong, right? she thought as she took out her hyperkinetic pistol and checked her aim on random targets.

HOKKI

Hokki had helped set up the hall of the new wing for the opening ceremony, not actually carrying anything, but giving his opinion about everything, like a true museum director. The new name of the wing shone in the sunlight, freshly repainted: "The Amazon Sisters-In-Arms Wing." He had come up with the idea himself, and, fortunately, it could easily be translated into Samarqandi. Inassa had congratulated him, given him a beautiful watch, and they had fucked after coming back from the restaurant. She hadn't mentioned anything about the international warrant against him, which was a relief.

Speaking of the devil, here she was, magnificent in a stunning red ensemble, with embroidery on the flaps of the jacket. Inassa waved her fingers at him when she spotted him.

"You've done a wonderful job, Hokki. You're really the man for this position. We're keeping you."

She winked at him and moved toward the bar, followed by a flock of bodyguards. Reassured for good this time, Hokki clapped his hands:

"Hurry, hurry! Get these last chairs into place. Their majesties will be arriving in a minute!"

KASSANDRA

Her poem reading had gone well, she was satisfied. She had written a shorter piece than she had planned, focused on war, death and love. Of course, she hadn't directly spoken of a sapphic relationship, but it was there, if you could read between the lines. Naila had whispered compliments in her ear when she had gone back to her seat under a thunderstorm of applause, followed by the cameras of the national TV channel, which was covering the event live. Naila's voice and her lips, so close to her neck, had made the hairs of Kassandra's arm rise. And her praise was the most valuable treasure of the day: she trusted Naila with all her heart. She was the best reader she had ever met—and the best lover. Of course, she would never tell Naila this. Love wasn't a gift; love was a bounty one had to struggle for. Like those Amazons. *Exactly* like those Amazons, as a matter of fact.

HOKKI

His ass hurt. The chairs were much less comfortable than they looked. He had to remember this for the next event. He applauded Princess Farah who had just finished her speech and watched Prince Hamad take his place behind the microphone. The king was still very sick, Hokki had been told, so he had sent his children to replace him. The princess had done a good job, from what Jalil, who was sitting right next to him, had translated. A burst of fireworks interrupted the crown prince's address, startling everybody. Something was thrown and exploded a few rows behind him. People screamed. More fireworks.

Chaos ensued. He saw cops shooting cops, bodies on the ground. Bodies! They were under attack. It was as if his brain lagged. Under attack! He turned to Jalil, but he wasn't there anymore. Then he saw him, lying face down, a red pool spreading around him. The volume of the noise was indescribable, and the room began to spin. Hokki was seized by panic, wanting everything to stop, everything to disappear, everything to be over. His instinct told him to run, but his legs gave under him, and he collapsed headfirst among the overturned chairs. A wonderful perfume filled his nostrils, making him smile before he lost consciousness.

KASSANDRA

Realizing with horror what was happening, Kassandra grabbed Naila's hand from behind and they both dropped to the ground. A grenade had exploded on the other side of the room. Naila was in a panic, making strange noises. She squeezed her hand, like with a child. There was more shooting. Bullets flew in all directions, like incredibly fast insects. She saw a figure walk toward them, shooting short bursts of its weapon. Naila whimpered higher. She had to protect her, protect her best reader, the love of her life. She flung herself on top of her lover, covering her body as best she could. The shadow was next to them now. Kassandra heard the man reload and shut her eyes tight. There was a deafening sound, a ripple of incredible punches on her back and then nothing, nothing at all, but the warm seeping of her blood over her lover's warm, trembling body.

ALI

Kneeling behind the illusory protection of a chair, Ali reloaded his gun. There was so much smoke around he couldn't distinguish anything. He was shooting at ghosts, hoping they were the right ones he was shooting at. He didn't know where the prince and the princess were, he didn't know if they were still alive, everything was pure chaos. His ears were filled with screams, detonations, absurd orders and incomprehensible words. A wave of despair overwhelmed him, and for a brief second, he felt like putting the gun into his own mouth. Then a couple of flash-bags exploded around him, deafening and blinding him at the same time. His gun fell on the floor, and he brought his hands to his ears. And that's when he saw it. The Golem. Rising high and tall among the smoke as the terrorists fell one by one, struck by its powerful hand. It grew and grew and grew, soon taller than the hall's ceiling, towering over the city without casting a shadow in the dazzling sunlight. Ali's eyes filled with tears, and he brought his right hand to his heart, as a humble, human, thank you. The doors blew open at this moment, and the antiterrorist units spread into the hall: a blue sea of weapons, shields and helmets.

Somebody grabbed him from behind and dragged him through the opened door.

"All clear!" he heard someone shout.

"All clear!" another yelled back.

Ali felt all his body begin to shake uncontrollably. He was still shaking in the ambulance, and he felt that it would never stop.

VITA

It took a few seconds for Vita to react when the attack began. The chaos was complete. The attackers were some officers from the security forces themselves, and they began by shooting at their colleagues, who shot back. A hand grenade was thrown, then flash-bangs and even a few smoke grenades. She couldn't see Kassandra from here. Hell, she almost couldn't see anything. Taking aim, Vitabegan shooting at all the officers with her silenced gun—she didn't have time to see who was a terrorist or not. She heard sirens howling outside and stepped down from the pedestal. Where was Kassandra? She moved swiftly between the chairs, looking around, peeking through the smoke, shooting down whatever threatening form she met. Finally, she discovered the body of the poetess, sprawled over Naila's, next to a terrorist Vita had just taken down.

I have failed, were the first words to cross her mind. *I'm so sorry, Kassandra. I have failed.*

A relative silence had finally fallen in the hall, and she looked around. People were standing back up, crying, choking because of the smoke, calling out names. The doors of the hall burst open, and the cavalry finally stomped in. She saw the prince and the princess being escorted outside. The storm-troopers were checking the building, yelling orders at each other.

Paramedics were checking the bodies, and Kassandra was removed on a stretcher.

Vita had failed. It wasn't the first time, but this time hurt the most. She liked that crazy woman. She even liked her poetry. What would Bruno say? How could she explain? She walked past the cops checking out the people in the hall and the paramedics hurrying in all directions. She walked, still invisible, in a city she felt she had doomed.

STAR
(EPILOGUE)

ALI

"So you found the king's will, finally," Ali said to Sekmet.

They were having an excellent supper in a restaurant in the old town, where his cousin had invited him. Ali was sure half of the customers were Bureau 23 agents. Sekmet shrugged.

"It was well hidden, but, yes, we managed to find it," he answered with a wink.

"And we have a queen now. Can I ask you . . . why did the king choose her?" the commissioner-general asked, using air quotes when he said "king."

Sekmet played with his glass of expensive wine, staring at its dark surface.

"Let's say that it's a bet," he said. "Maybe this city really needs to move on. The king started it. Queen Farah wants to pursue this direction. Many powerful people do too."

"You mean, like the local energy industry?" Ali said, with an ironic smile.

"Among others," Sekmet agreed.

Ali put down his fork and knife and wiped his lips with a very white towel.

"We fucked up," he said. "We both really did. I don't understand how we kept our jobs. I'm serious. In the old days, we would be both rotting in prison."

Sekmet bent over his plate and spoke in a low voice.

"It always helps to be good friends with a future queen," he said.

Ali nodded. "Indeed."

He frowned and this time it was his turn to bend over his own plate. "Can you do me a favor, then?"

Sekmet shrugged. "We've already done you a huge favor, cousin. I'm not sure it would be wise to ask for more."

"It's not for me. It's for my friend, the political refugee from Viborg City. I want you to protect him. I'm afraid he would be a problem for the queen's diplomacy, regarding the Western Alliance."

Sekmet looked at his cousin, as if he was evaluating him.

"What do I get in exchange?"

"The complete list of our informants. The full files."

"That would work," the Secret Service official said. "And in return, we erase our files on this guy, as if he never came to our city. Impossible to trace."

"Thank you," Ali said. "I'll send you the passwords to access the files tomorrow."

They raised their glasses, clinking edges lightly. A tiny, crystalline note briefly rose in the air, beautiful and ephemeral. *Like this friendship*, Ali thought. *Like this friendship.*

NAILA

I have just visited you in the hospital. You looked good, given the circumstances. I brought you flowers—your favorite, white lilies. Always the romantic at heart. We chatted for a short while, you laughed a little, I showed you the official award letter the Clarice Lispector Award committee sent you. You said you didn't care, but I know you do. I will have it framed tomorrow, so it can hang in our dining room. You will probably say you hate it, but I don't care. Because I know you love me. You saved my life, protected me with your body. The scars that will remain on your back will each be a small heart bearing our invisible initials. I love you too, as you very well know, and I will keep protecting you. You will never know it, but I will. Every evening, when I write my report, I will lie and protect you. It will remain my secret. My not-so-dirty secret. I am your invisible armor and, like our love, it is indestructible.

THOMAS

Thomas turned off the alarm, and realized Saran wasn't next to him in the bed.

"You're up early again," he said, walking into the kitchen where Saran was sitting, drinking her strong tea in front of her laptop.

"I have a big meeting this morning," she explained. "And the new minister of culture himself will be there. I can't fuck up."

"When have you ever fucked up in your job?" Thomas asked, pouring himself a large glass of tea.

Saran shrugged without answering. The guy who had replaced her at the head of the National Museum scientific department had been sacked after the new queen had come to power, and Saran had been reinstated, with a raise. Her former boss was now the queen's personal advisor, and this might have explained it, although Thomas wanted to think that it was only thanks to his wife's talents.

"I have to go!" she said, shutting the laptop. She stood up and they kissed, a little longer than usual.

Maybe we'll really live happily ever after, he thought as she slammed the door behind her. *Or at least, for a while.*

HOKKI

Hokki opened the large bay window of his new apartment and stepped onto the balcony overlooking the busy streets of New Samarqand. Inassa had told him she had personally chosen it for him, and he had to admit she had good taste. It was within walking distance of the National Museum, in the posh district of the city. He had discovered a few very nice restaurants and cafés.

He thought about Jalil and felt a small pinch in his heart. He sure was an annoying dude, but he only meant well. Hokki didn't know for sure, but it seemed that Jalil had taken the bullet that was destined for Hokki—at least that was what his conscience told him. He had escaped the attack miraculously unhurt, maybe because he had fainted, making the terrorists think he was dead.

Since Jalil's death, he didn't have a bodyguard anymore as the political situation seemed to have stabilized since the new queen had stepped into office. The new wing was a success, nationally and internationally—the local media had turned the possible love story of the two female warriors into a tale of "strong camaraderie," in which they had died side by side defending Samarqand against foreign invaders. Walking back into his spacious sitting room, Hokki looked at the pink phone resting on a shelf. Nobody had asked him to give it back, and he had no intention of doing so. It was a relic that would always remind him that yes, miracles could happen, but that they never, ever erased the tragic events they were connected to.

VITA

Packing her stuff was quick business. Travel light, essential rule. She walked down the stairs of the hotel, left the key on the counter and hopped on her motorcycle. Bruno had given her a new assignment, a new passport and a plane ticket. She hadn't totally fucked up. At least, that's what he had said. "It's like the Tao," he had told her, sitting on her bed while she dyed her hair blonde in the sink. "Sometimes, good comes from bad—and vice-versa. Not only had Kassandra survived, but she now has even more visibility. And we both know she is anything but mainstream. Now she can yell with a megaphone ten thousand times louder than before. And that will surely annoy the Empire . . . So, don't blame yourself. Things happen you can't control. Don't let them control you. That's the secret to remaining focused."

Bruno was also pleased with the alliance they had officially formed with the Egregorian Society. Vita had given Thomas a small bag of Synth that he could distribute. The more Synthers, the stronger they would be.

She turned and followed the avenue that would take her to the airport.

In the deep blue sky, she knew the Dark Shield satellite, the Subliminal Empire's electronic spy, was trying to locate her and her allies. But Synth made them invisible to their radar. Synth made them invincible.

She gave her motorcycle more gas and zoomed past the other cars.

Focused. She was totally focused.

About the Author

Seb Doubinsky is an award-winning bilingual writer born in Paris in 1963. His novels, all set in a dystopian universe revolving around competing city-states, have been published in the UK and in the USA, and translated into numerous languages. He currently lives with his family in Aarhus, Denmark, where he teaches at the university.

DID YOU ENJOY THIS BOOK?

If so, word-of-mouth recommendations and online reviews are critical to the success of any book, so we hope you'll tell your friends about it and consider leaving a review at your favorite bookseller's or library's website.

Visit us at www.meerkatpress.com for our full catalog.

Meerkat Press
Asheville